A Fall of
Secrets

A Shade of Vampire, Book 15

Bella Forrest

A SHADE OF KIEV TRILOGY:

A Shade of Kiev 1
A Shade of Kiev 2
A Shade of Kiev 3

BEAUTIFUL MONSTER DUOLOGY:

Beautiful Monster 1
Beautiful Monster 2

For an updated list of Bella's books,
please visit www.bellaforrest.net

Contents

Chapter 1: Rhys

We had to collect a large amount of human blood—larger than ever before—and we had to do it quickly. Thanks to the Novak boy, at least we didn't need to keep our activities hidden now. This was the only thing that made our task less daunting.

I had given all our witches an hour to recuperate after the battle. I headed straight to Isolde's rooms at the top of the castle and hurried toward her bedroom where she lay resting, cradling an injured elbow. Burns covered every visible part of her skin, as with Julisse and I. But burns were the least of our worries right now.

She looked up at me, the torture of the setback we'd

just experienced still fresh in her eyes.

I brushed aside my own disappointment, and touched her shoulder.

"Will you be able to accompany us?"

She nodded, reaching for a glass of wolf blood by the side of her bed and taking a deep gulp. She wiped her mouth against the back of her sleeve. "I've been thinking carefully about this next step," she said, her voice hoarse. "Since we don't have much time, we need to be very precise in our targeting."

"I'm listening," I said.

"Young blood is what we need. It will be at least four, possibly five times more effective than adult blood. We ought to target adolescents."

I nodded. "I will plan a route accordingly."

I walked over to my aunt's desk in the corner of the room, reached up to a shelf above it, and pulled down a map. I began paging through it until I reached one of the nearest inhabited shorelines to us. Isolde slid out of bed and walked over to me, looking down at the map from behind my shoulder.

"We still have some werewolves back in our dungeon on the other side of the gate. If we have time, we could also collect some more wolves from their realm… And there are also a few humans left in our dungeon, but they're mostly shriveled and sickly by now."

"Hm," I grunted, barely paying attention to her words as I pulled out a pen from the drawer and began making markings on the map. "I have our route now," I said, tearing out the page from the map, folding it, and slipping it into my cloak pocket. I walked into the bathroom and stopped in front of the sink, splashing cold water over my face. I raised my head and looked at myself in the mirror. The words Mona had spoken to me echoed through my head.

She said that I looked older.

I shook thoughts of that witch away and dried my hands and face with a towel before re-entering Isolde's bedroom. She had finished the last of the wolf blood and was fastening a cloak around her.

"How is your elbow?" I asked.

"Better now that I've finished that," my aunt replied, nodding toward the empty glass.

We vanished ourselves down to the entrance hall at the bottom of the castle, where all our other capable witches, including Julisse, were waiting for us.

Julisse shot me a questioning glance. "Have you decided on our first destination?"

I nodded. I didn't want to waste time explaining where. They would find out soon enough. We all formed a circle, touching shoulders, and disappeared from the spot.

Moments later, we had reappeared at the side of a dusty road. The sun blazed down overhead, reflecting off the cars whizzing past us. I pointed to the gate on the opposite pavement. As my companions looked at it, they all seemed to understand. We crossed the road quickly, not even bothering to conceal ourselves with an invisibility spell, and approached the gate. I peered through the bars, pleased to see so many of our targets all in one place. One schoolyard.

We reappeared on the other side of the gate. I looked over the crowd of teenagers. Some had noticed us already and were eyeing us curiously. Most were still too wrapped up talking.

Three adults who'd been conversing in a corner noticed us too late. I had already released three curses. Each hit them square in the chest. They collapsed to the ground dead in a heap.

The youth began to shout. We needed to act fast now if we wanted to avoid delays. The last thing we needed was for humans with guns to show up and complicate matters. We surrounded the crowd of adolescents, ushering them closer and closer into the center of the yard with a burning ring of fire. The heat made them retreat quickly and soon they were so close together that their shoulders were touching. Confident they were compact enough, I nodded toward the other witches and relinquished the fire.

A few seconds later, we had vanished along with our first batch of young blood.

Chapter 2: Rose

I woke to Caleb's strong arms around me. He hadn't stopped holding me since we'd fallen asleep. I stared into his peaceful face. His breathing was light, his lips slightly parted. I leaned toward him on the pillow and planted a soft kiss on his forehead. Slowly, his eyelids flickered open. His lips curved, his warm brown eyes lighting up. Caleb's smile was the only sunrise I needed.

"How did you sleep?" I asked.

He responded by pulling me closer and claiming my lips.

I chuckled as he drew away. "I'll take that as well."

He sat up and looked at the clock in the corner of

the room.

"We've slept too long," he muttered.

"Oh, my," I said, my eyes traveling to the clock too. "We have." We had been through so much in the past twenty-four hours, and we'd both needed to rest, but neither of us had intended to remain in bed this long. More than six hours had passed.

We climbed out of bed and headed to the bathroom. After we'd finished brushing our teeth, Caleb stripped and stepped into the shower. I left my own clothes aside and followed after him. The water felt strangely cool. I adjusted the taps, adding more hot water.

Caleb backed away from the water. "That's hot."

I frowned, looking back at the taps. It barely felt warm to me. "Sorry," I muttered, adjusting the shower to its former temperature.

Caleb moved behind me again, positioning himself beneath the water, and ran his palms down my arms. "Your body's changed. You barely notice heat."

"Hmm... I guess. Speaking of heat, do you think the dragons have left already?"

"I assume so," he replied. "They said they'd leave after they'd finished meeting with your parents."

Once we'd finished, we stepped out of the shower, dried off and got dressed.

"Let's go see my parents," I said.

Exiting the cabin, I breathed deeply as the fresh mountain air whipped past my face. Something was very different about our surroundings. Dotted about the mountainside were dozens more cabins than there had been when Caleb and I had first retreated into our own. And they were larger than the regular cabins constructed for the witches. As we began to make our way down the mountainside, I spotted Micah and Kira seated on the steps of a cabin about fifty feet away from our own. They were staring out at the view of the ocean, their arms around each other.

"Micah!" I called.

Micah beamed as we hurried over to them. I still wasn't sure whether the wolf had sensed me eavesdropping when he'd finally professed his love for Kira on the beach, so I tried to look surprised to see them both together.

"So, you two are a couple now?"

Micah's cheeks reddened as he nodded, looking down affectionately at Kira.

"Congratulations," Caleb said, even as he cast me an amused sideways glance.

"And now we are neighbors." I frowned, confused as I took in all the extra mountain cabins. "I thought the werewolves were going to be housed up in the trees along with the vampires?"

"That was the plan," Micah said, "but we soon realized that it's going to be much more practical to house us in cabins. When we're in our wolf forms, even ascending in an elevator can be inconvenient." He looked down at his now human hands. "It's hard to push buttons with paws."

"Do you know if the witches have finished with construction around the rest of the island?" I asked.

Micah shrugged. "I think these cabins were one of the first projects they worked on. But Kira and I haven't had a chance to roam around the island much in the past few hours. We've been…resting."

"Okay," I said. "Well, we're going to visit my parents now. We'll see you around."

We bade them goodbye before continuing down the mountain. Caleb motioned to pick me up as soon as we reached the bottom, but I clutched his hands and stopped him.

"I want to see if I can match your speed," I said.

Caleb looked at me in confusion. I realized then that he hadn't witnessed my speed since my fire powers came on.

"I noticed it soon after I discovered I was able to

wield fire," I said, taking a step back from him, casting my eyes toward the entrance to the woods. "My speed has increased. A lot. I'm just not sure how much exactly." I narrowed my eyes on him in challenge. "So, vampire, race me?"

I didn't wait for an answer before launching into a sprint across the field. I'd guessed Caleb would overtake me in a matter of seconds. He did. But he didn't outpace me as much as I'd expected. I was still nowhere near as fast as him, but as he reached the finish line, I was only about twelve feet behind him. Not bad going against a runner like Caleb Achilles.

He stopped at the entrance to the forest, and turned around, watching as I ran the last few feet toward him. He raised a brow.

"I'm impressed," he said.

When I pulled to a stop, I wasn't even panting. It was a bizarre feeling. I had often fantasized about running this fast as a child. I recalled in my early childhood years being fascinated watching the vampires whizz effortlessly through the trees. Ben and I used to attempt to match them—attempts that ended up with more bumps and bruises than we could count.

Fire-wielder. Speed runner. I can live with this.

"It looks like you won't have to carry me around as

much now," I said.

Caleb looked almost disappointed.

"What's wrong?" I asked.

He shook his head, smiling. "It's nothing... I suppose I'm just old-fashioned. I've come to enjoy carrying you around."

I couldn't help but giggle. "You can still carry me around if you want, Caleb." I wrapped my arms around his midriff and drew him in for a kiss.

He slipped his right arm beneath my knees, his left arm wrapping around my waist as he picked me up and carried me against him. He brushed his lips against my forehead and I held on tight, preparing myself for him to begin lurching forward through the forest. The truth was, although I could run fast myself now, I loved this *old-fashioned* side of Caleb. It was endearing and romantic.

It wasn't long before we reached the foot of my parents' tree. Caleb didn't bother waiting for the elevator. With one giant leap, he hurtled us both upward toward the canopy of leaves. I was gasping for breath as we finally landed on the veranda. He set me down on my feet and we walked toward the front door. I knocked.

No answer.

I knocked again. Still no answer.

I wondered if they were perhaps sleeping. I walked along the wooden floorboards toward the kitchen window, which was ajar. *I should have remembered to keep a spare key.*

I opened the window further and called inside. "Mom? Dad?"

When there was still no answer I looked back at Caleb.

"I think we're going to have to climb through the window," I said.

"You think they're sleeping?" Caleb asked.

I shrugged. "I don't know."

Caleb supported my feet and helped lift me up on to the windowsill. I climbed inside, over the counter, and lowered myself onto the floor. I called for my parents again. I entered the living room. It was empty. I headed straight for my parents' bedroom. I placed my ear against the door. Sure enough, I heard light breathing. They were both sound asleep. I wasn't used to my parents being such deep sleepers. As vampires, they were easy to wake. But, like Caleb and myself, they were exhausted after the battle. I headed toward the front door. Picking up a spare key on the way out, I re-entered the veranda. Caleb was leaning against the railing.

"They're both asleep," I said. "Let's return in an hour. In the meantime, we can see for ourselves what improvements have been done on the island since we last saw it."

We headed back down the tree and went first to the Port. I was half expecting to see the same scene of destruction that I'd laid eyes on only hours ago. But I shouldn't have been surprised. Our witches had been working hard. What had previously been a scene of destruction—a landscape of nothing but lumps of ash and black charcoal—was now a fully reconstructed port, hardly different from the one that used to stand here. Even the jetty was made of the same type of wood, and the sand on the beach was back to its light golden color and soft texture. While the affected trees hadn't re-sprouted, the burnt timber had been cleared away. I was just thankful that the majority of our forests remained intact. *Thank God I attracted those dragons' attention when I did.* If I hadn't, the whole island would have been burnt to the ground.

Caleb and I began walking further up the beach that had borne the brunt of the attack. Caleb pointed to a patch of sand to our left. "That was where the witches lined up their prisoners," he said, his eyes distant. "I honestly thought we'd lost them."

"Thank heavens those witches saw enough value in them to keep them."

Caleb averted his gaze to the ocean. "If it weren't for your father, I wouldn't be standing here now. Rhys almost finished me off."

I shuddered, tightening my grip around his hand.

Sensing my discomfort, Caleb changed the subject. "We still don't know how Mona ended up in the middle of the lake..." Caleb's voice trailed off as his eyes fixed on something in the waves. He pointed toward a large round object bobbing in the distance. I squinted as we hurried closer to the water's edge.

"What do you think it is?" I asked, anxiety gripping me.

"Oh... It's just the ogre."

"Brett?"

Caleb nodded. "It looks like he's bathing."

I strained to make him out in the distance. Now that we were closer, it did appear as though he was cleaning himself. I hadn't even known that ogres could swim and I certainly hadn't known that they cleaned themselves. It sure didn't smell like it...

Caleb and I were about to move on when one of his thick hands shot up into the air and began waving at us.

"Princess Rose!" he bellowed. "Hello!"

"Hi, Brett," I yelled back.

He began swimming toward us until he was in shallow enough water to stand up. I gasped, thinking for one horrifying moment that he was wearing no clothes. His massive chest was bare, rolls of flab drooping around his stomach. Then to my relief, I noticed a loincloth on his waist as he stepped onto the sand.

"How are you?" I asked.

He shrugged his shoulders.

"How are you getting along with Bella?"

He shrugged again.

"Have you talked much since I introduced the two of you?"

"Not much," Brett mumbled.

"Are you glad she's here?" It felt like trying to draw blood out of a stone.

He looked down at his massive feet, shuffling from one to the other. "I don't know…" I could have sworn I detected a slight blush in his muddy brown cheeks.

"I think she likes you," I said.

Truth be told, I had no idea whether Bella liked Brett. I just wanted to see whether the blush I thought I'd detected was real.

There it was again. A slight warming to his cheeks.

"Is she mean like other girl ogres?" I asked.

He shrugged again. "I give her my food, so… that's why she's not mean."

While I was amused by Brett's take on Bella, I couldn't help but be saddened too. I could only imagine what he'd been through at the hands of other ogres.

I frowned at the ogre in mock disdain. I shook my head. "You should consider the possibility that she might like you for more than just your cooking."

He let out a deep sigh that rumbled through his chest and made the flab around his stomach shake. He shook his head, then turned his gaze toward the sea.

I didn't want to make the ogre any more uncomfortable than I had already, so I looped my arm through Caleb's and said, "Well, I will see you around, Brett."

"Bye, Princess Rose," Brett mumbled, still avoiding eye contact as he began trundling back toward the direction of his cave.

Caleb and I spent the rest of the hour exploring the parts of the island that had been most affected by the dragons' flames. Like the Port, most other places had been restored. After we were done touring the island, we headed back to my parents' apartment. We ascended in the elevator and, arriving on the veranda, I let us in through the front door. This time, my parents were both seated at the dining table in the kitchen. They both looked up as we entered.

"Rose!" My mother beckoned me over.

Caleb and I took seats around the dining table. "You two must have been tired," I said. "We came by earlier."

My father let out a yawn.

"I guess the dragons left already?" I asked.

"Oh, yes," my father replied, rubbing his face in his hands. "They left some hours ago."

"When will they return?" Caleb asked.

"They didn't specify," my father replied. "I don't imagine they will be away long though. They are fetching their prince and about fifty other dragons."

"And what about their accommodations?" I asked.

"The witches are working on them now. We are converting the storage chambers into apartments for the dragons. They said they like high ceilings and the rooms we had built for humans simply won't do," my mother said. "We're holding a memorial ceremony for our fallen in an hour. I'm going to take a quick shower." She stood up and headed out of the room.

I reached across the table and gripped my father's forearm. "Thank you for saving Caleb."

My father nodded, glancing briefly at Caleb.

The three of us didn't exchange many more words until my mother reappeared from her shower dressed in a long black robe. I looked down at my own clothes, then at Caleb's. We ought to change into something more subdued too. I took Caleb's hand and walked with him toward my bedroom. I didn't have any long black dresses like my mother's, so instead I pulled out a smart black shirt and pants, followed by a long black cardigan. I slipped into them quickly before leaving the room again and entering Ben's bedroom with Caleb. I searched through my brother's closet until I found a black outfit for Caleb as well. He changed quickly and we returned to the living room. My father had also changed into black clothes.

We all left the apartment together and headed towards the Sanctuary. People—humans, vampires, witches and werewolves alike—were already gathering in the clearing outside of the witches' temple. Since we had no bodies to bury, we held a similar ceremony to the one we'd tried to hold for my own grandfather and those we'd mistakenly thought we'd lost.

Corrine was standing in the center of the courtyard, arranging row upon row of burning candles. More and more people were arriving by the moment. We all took a candle and returned to our spots around the courtyard. Once the area was filled to capacity, Corrine floated the remaining candles higher in the sky until they were all hovering above our heads.

One by one, the relatives of our fallen stepped up by the fountain and spoke eulogies. My eyes glossed over as I stared into the flickering flame of my candle. I should have been grateful that we hadn't lost more of our people. After all, every single one of us should have burnt to the ground last night. But all I felt was sadness and remorse.

However, as the ceremony neared a close, I dried my tears and a different emotion took hold of me. Hope. That from this day forward, The Shade would be a safer place.

Chapter 3: Aiden

I had been avoiding Adelle all throughout the ceremony, not that it was difficult. She had been avoiding me too. I didn't catch her once looking my way. Perhaps she felt embarrassed.

The redheaded witch had been playing on my mind ever since she'd come to see me. I couldn't deny that I was still deeply attracted to her. But the werewolf had gotten under my skin, touched me in ways that I hadn't expected. She truly was a breath of fresh air. After Camilla, Kailyn's frankness and straightforwardness were qualities I needed in a life partner. Kailyn was everything that Camilla wasn't. And though physically she wasn't my type, somehow I preferred that she wasn't. Adelle's beauty was almost too similar to Camilla's for comfort. It felt like Kailyn was the clean break I needed in life. In love.

Although I'd known Adelle for much longer, I couldn't be sure that her attachment to me was as true as Kailyn's. Granted, I had certainly taken my time in asking her out, but if she had truly had a crush on me all those years, what had been stopping her from expressing her feelings? I wondered whether it was more the breakdown in our friendship since she'd started going out with Eli than actual love for me that had caused her to react the way she had.

But whatever was going on in that witch's head, I was Kailyn's now.

After the ceremony, Kailyn and I made our way back to our mountain cabin. Although we could have opted to live in the trees, I'd realized that it would be much more practical to stay in the cabin when Kailyn transformed into a wolf. We walked hand in hand up the cabin steps, in through the front door and dropped down on the sofa in the living room. She wrapped an arm around my waist and leaned her head against my chest. I stroked her wavy blonde hair, resting my lips against her head.

"Sometimes I wish I could turn you into a werewolf," she said with a smile.

"Why's that?" I asked.

"Werewolves just have more fun."

I chuckled. "You're probably right."

"Though," she said, "it's true that vampires have one advantage over us. They live forever."

I hadn't thought until now about the longevity of werewolves. "How long do werewolves live?" I asked.

"A long time. But not forever."

I held her hand and kissed it. "Well, a very long time will have to be good enough for me. Unless we can turn you into a vampire."

She smiled. "I'm not even sure that wolves can turn into vampires. Perhaps it's something that could be done with the assistance of the black witches... But honestly, I'm not sure I could handle being so cold all the time."

"You get used to it," I said grimly.

"Hey, Aiden!" a familiar voice called from outside the cabin.

I walked over to the door and opened it. Claudia stood on my doorstep, hands on her hips.

I raised a brow. "What brings you here, Mrs. Lazaroff?"

She cast a fleeting glance over my shoulder into the cabin and waved at Kailyn. "Hi, Kailyn," she said.

The wolf appeared at my side. She gave Claudia a smile. "Hello."

Claudia looked back at me. "Well, as you know, Yuri and I have some… business to do."

She paused.

"And?" I prompted.

"And it means that not only will he and I turn back into humans, we're going to leave this island for a while. Like Xavier and Vivienne, Yuri and I didn't ever have a proper honeymoon. We were stuck on this island as vampires."

"When will you turn?"

"Tomorrow morning. We'll take the cure and leave right afterward—assuming we recover quickly. So… I wanted to invite you round now, to catch up on a few things and to say goodbye."

"Oh, I see." I looked down at Kailyn. "Would you like to come?"

Claudia cleared her throat. "Yuri wanted to have a bit of private time with you. You know, man to man."

Kailyn was quick to pick up on the hint. "You go, Aiden. I'll stay here, or I might even go to my sister's cabin to see how she's settling in with Micah."

"Okay, I'll meet you back here in a while."

I gave her a hug before setting off with Claudia down the mountainside. I cast her a curious glance. "Man to man?"

"Well, I'll be in on the conversation too but…" Her voice trailed off. "Kailyn," she mouthed silently. I had no idea why the couple would want to talk to me about Kailyn. But now wasn't the time to press. We had to reach the treehouse, where we would be far enough from Kailyn for there to be too many other noises for her to distinguish our voices.

We reached the couple's treehouse in a matter of minutes. Entering through the doorway, Claudia called out, "Baby."

Yuri strolled into the entryway. He gave me a smile before leading us into the living room and sitting down on the couch, gesturing that I do the same. I sat down in an armchair opposite him while Claudia sat next to him.

"Glad you could make it," Yuri said.

"Claudia tells me you're leaving the island tomorrow."

"That's the plan." Yuri placed an arm around Claudia's shoulder.

"Where will you go?"

Claudia's face lit up. She placed a tender kiss on Yuri's cheek. "We didn't want to be copycats and go to Greece like Xavier and Vivienne. So I convinced Yuri to take me to Paris."

"Paris?"

"Uh-huh." Claudia nodded, a huge grin on her face. "My father was a Frenchman. And Yuri has French roots too, on his mother's side."

I couldn't help but chuckle. I could just imagine Claudia prancing along a Parisian boulevard, bags of shopping dangling from her arms as she dragged Yuri along behind her.

I gave Yuri a broad smile. "Make sure you bring enough cash."

"Yeah," he muttered.

"Anyway," Claudia said, "I didn't just call you here to say goodbye. I wanted to talk to you about Adelle."

I groaned internally. "What about Adelle?"

Claudia exchanged glances with Yuri. "She's broken up with Eli."

"What?"

Yuri nodded.

"Why?" My mouth hung open.

"From what I managed to get out of Eli," Claudia said, "she didn't give a reason. She just said she felt that they needed a break… But I have a theory. I think she broke up with Eli because of you."

I narrowed my eyes on Claudia. "What makes you say that?"

She shrugged. "Just intuition, I guess…"

I let out a groan. The last thing I wanted was for Adelle to break up with Eli. I'd been devastated when they'd first gotten together, but since I'd met Kailyn, I'd grown to feel pleased for the couple. Eli deserved happiness just as much as I did.

"That's why you didn't want Kailyn here," I muttered.

Claudia nodded.

I ran a hand through my hair. "I'm not sure why you're telling me this. Adelle doesn't concern me anymore. You know I'm with Kailyn."

"I just thought you ought to know," Claudia said.

I stood up from the armchair and walked over to the window. I stared out at the tree branches. "I loved Adelle for years," I said softly. "There was nothing stopping her from approaching me if she'd felt the same."

"Well, witches are different than wolves," Claudia said. "They're more traditional."

I exhaled sharply. "I'm with Kailyn now." I realized

that I was repeating myself. I was saying this more to myself than to anyone else.

I'm with Kailyn. She's right for me.

I turned around again to look at the couple. "So was that all you wanted to tell me?"

Claudia nodded, looking at me with a pained expression on her face.

Yuri stood up and, walking over to me, gripped my shoulder. "Personally, I think Kailyn's the right choice."

I nodded curtly. "Well, I hope the cure goes smoothly. And if you are leaving tomorrow, let me know. I'd like to see you off at the Port."

I walked toward the door.

"Bye, honey," Claudia said.

"Bye."

As I left that treehouse and descended back down to the forest floor, Yuri's words replayed in my mind.

Kailyn's the right choice.

Kailyn's the right choice.

CHAPTER 4: MONA

I returned with Kiev to our new residence—a grand treehouse not too far away from Derek and Sofia's. This was the first time we'd even laid eyes on it since the witches had erected it. We walked slowly from room to room, starting with the beautifully furnished living room, moving on to the kitchen, the dining room, and then the three bedrooms. Ibrahim and Corrine could have made it larger for us, but I'd requested that they keep it small. Neither Kiev nor I liked huge homes. We were much happier in more contained spaces. It wasn't like we were expecting to have many guests stay over anyway.

As we entered the master bedroom, I sat down on the edge of the king-sized bed. Kiev walked over to the window and looked out before turning around to face me.

"What do you think?" I asked.

He shrugged. "Looks good enough."

I nodded. My eyes fell to his prosthetic arm. Although having a missing arm didn't seem to bother Kiev, it still pained me every time I looked at it. It reminded me what he'd sacrificed for me. For us. I rolled the engagement ring on my finger.

"What's wrong?" Kiev frowned. "Don't you like this place?"

"I love it." I gave him a watery smile. I reached for his right arm and pulled him down on the bed to sit next to me. Cupping his face with my hands, I brushed my thumbs against his rough cheeks. I closed my eyes. "I love you, Kiev," I whispered, biting my lip.

He reached for my chin and pressed his lips against mine in a firm yet tender kiss. Then, holding me by the waist with his left arm, he raised my hand and kissed the ring. His voice husky, he looked me deep in the eyes. "Let's get married, Mona," he said. "Before things get crazy again, I want to make you my bride."

Butterflies fluttered in my stomach. Although I

wanted nothing more than to accept Kiev's suggestion, I couldn't help but feel it was too soon, too close to the funeral ceremony. Too close to the destruction we'd just been through. "Do you really think now is the right time for a wedding?"

He wet his lower lip, his expression concerned. "We don't know when we'll get another chance. If there's one thing I've learned while staying on this island, it's that if there's anything you want to do, you need to do it at the first opportunity. Anything can happen at any time in The Shade."

He lifted himself off the bed, pulling me up into a standing position next to him. Sliding both hands around my waist, he pulled me flush against his body, bending me back gently and trailing kisses down my throat.

"Let's get married, Mona," he said again.

"Okay," I breathed. "Let's get married."

Barely had I said the words before he scooped me up in his arms and began racing toward the exit of the apartment. Running out onto the balcony, he leapt up onto the railing and with one giant leap almost gave me a heart attack as we hurtled down to the ground. I was winded as we landed, practically strangling him with my grip.

"Wh-Where are you taking me?"

"We ought to let the Novaks know first."

After recovering from the drop, I couldn't help but laugh at the speed at which he was running. The wind blew so violently against me I could barely keep my eyes open. "You know, I could just magic us there."

Kiev smiled but didn't take me up on my suggestion.

"I have no idea how to organize a wedding." I'd spent too many years of my life believing that I might never even have a wedding. "I'm sure Corrine can help us though."

As we reached Derek and Sofia's treehouse, Kiev didn't bother knocking. The door had been left unlocked and he was able to push it wide open.

Sofia came hurrying into the living room at the noise.

"Kiev? Mona? What are you doing here?"

"We want to get married," Kiev stated calmly.

Sofia looked only mildly surprised. "Oh… When?"

"Tomorrow," Kiev replied.

"Kiev," I said, "do you have any idea how much work goes into a wedding?"

He cocked his head to one side and looked down at me. "Do you?"

Sofia chuckled. "We'll manage it, I'm sure. The way

things have been going on this island recently, I don't blame you for wanting to get it done as soon as possible. Corrine is the best at weddings around here, as you may already know. I suggest going to see her and starting the arrangements."

"Thanks, Sofia," I said, before Kiev carried me back out of the apartment.

"Since we don't have much time now," I said, "let me just magic us to Corrine's."

Kiev acquiesced and a few seconds later, we were standing outside the Sanctuary. I knocked on the door. Corrine answered a few moments later. Her expression was sober after the ceremony she'd just led us through. The last thing I felt like talking to her about was our wedding. Still, it seemed that we were going through with this.

"Kiev and I want to take advantage of this downtime and get married."

I felt relieved when her face lit up a little. She smiled and gripped my hand, pulling me inside. "Come in, come in. This island could do with a wedding after all this heaviness."

She led Kiev and me into the living room and we all took seats. I could tell after about fifteen minutes that Kiev regretted being included in the meeting. He got up and began walking around the room, examining objects on the mantelpiece, as Corrine and I discussed details for the next hour.

He looked relieved when we had finished. Corrine smirked as she looked at Kiev.

"So, Kiev. You're really ready to tie the knot?"

He rolled his eyes. "Have you two finished?"

I nodded.

"Then let's go," Kiev said, heading toward the door.

Corrine cleared her throat. "Go where exactly, vampire? Mona and I might be finished with each other, but we haven't even started with you."

"What?" He looked at us.

"You obviously weren't paying attention to our conversation. We've got our work cut out if we want you to be even a half-presentable groom for Mona."

Kiev looked himself over. "What work?" He narrowed his eyes on the witch.

"The fact that you can't even see what work needs to be done on you shows just how much we have to do," Corrine replied, furrowing her brows and folding her arms over her chest. "I don't even trust Ibrahim to tidy you up. I'm going to have to deal with you myself."

I chuckled silently at Kiev's scowl. He wasn't in that scruffy a state. But as I caught the teasing spark in

Corrine's eyes, something told me that she was going to enjoy "tidying up" Kiev more than the actual wedding.

Chapter 5: Mona

Corrine was true to her word in taking over Kiev's preparation. In the meantime, she paired me with another witch, Leyni. I spent the rest of the day with Leyni preparing my outfit and doing a hair and makeup rehearsal. In the evening, she guided me through a number of beauty treatments.

It was late by the time we'd finished. Kiev still hadn't returned. Corrine had wanted to keep us separate until the wedding. I wasn't sure how much time exactly the witch had ended up spending on him—I suspected not all that long, since she had a lot of work to do in arranging the actual event. Although I missed lying in

Kiev's arms that night, I found amusement in imagining where Corrine was putting him up for the night. I was sure that she still hadn't forgiven him for the night he'd stolen Ben Novak from her arms. And although Kiev was sorry, Corrine still liked to dig her heels in when she could, albeit in a good-natured way.

I woke up the next morning to find Leyni already running a bath for me.

"Come on, Sleeping Beauty," she called. "We've got a lot to do before the wedding starts at noon."

I slid out of bed and entered the bathroom. I didn't spend long in the bath—Leyni was already knocking on the door after less than twenty minutes had passed. I got out and dried myself before dressing and starting makeup and hair. I wasn't sure why I was suddenly so nervous.

Leyni must have noticed. She placed an arm on my shoulder and gave me a warm smile.

"It's normal to feel tense on the morning of your wedding. But don't worry. Everything will go smoothly."

The next few hours passed quickly until finally, I was staring at myself in the mirror, fully dressed and made up. The dress we'd designed together was stunning. Long-sleeved, it had a heart-shaped neckline and complemented my curves perfectly. She had curled my hair into gentle waves and braided it with small pink flowers.

"Well," Leyni said, eyeing me with pride. "Let's go."

I nodded, drawing a breath.

She held my hand and we vanished from the spot. When my vision came into focus again, we were standing a dozen feet back from a crowd that had formed on the beach near the Port. There were rows upon rows of chairs with an aisle in between, at the end of which was a raised platform decorated with white roses and silk drapes. Kiev already stood on the platform, Matteo by his side as best man.

Leyni stepped in front of me and lowered the veil over my face. She gave me a smirk. "Vampires have good eyesight. We don't want your groom sneaking a peek at you yet."

"Mona," a chorus of voices called behind me.

I turned to see Rose hurrying toward me with half a dozen other young women. They all wore light pink dresses and held bunches of flowers in their hands. My bridesmaids. Rose handed me a bouquet of dark blue lilies. My voice caught in my throat at the sight of them. They reminded me so much of the lilies that grew around my lake house back on our old island.

Memories of the time I'd spent there with Kiev soon after we'd first met washed over me.

Rose squeezed my hand. "You look incredible. How are you feeling?"

I caught a tear at the corner of my eye before it could slip down my cheek. I beamed down at Rose. "I've never been better."

Once Rose and another bridesmaid had picked up the hem of my dress, Leyni looped her arm through mine and we began walking down the aisle between the chairs. I looked around at everyone who'd come to attend. There were too many faces to count—vampires, werewolves and humans. I kept my eyes anywhere but straight ahead until I reached five rows away from the platform. Finally, I allowed myself to look up.

Ibrahim was now standing in the center of the platform, and to his right was Kiev. Matteo stood a few feet behind him. I couldn't help but grin. I'd never seen Kiev looking so smart. He was almost unrecognizable. He wore a crisp black tuxedo and his hair was neatly combed back away from his face. His stubble had been trimmed right down, so only shadow was visible around his jawline. His skin also looked brighter somehow, as though he might have had a facial, and I could barely notice his prosthetic arm. His eyes were glued on me, as

I was sure they had been ever since I started walking down the aisle.

My grip around Leyni's arm tightened. Although this was the happiest moment of my life, I couldn't help but feel a stab of melancholy that it wasn't my father walking beside me.

Reaching the foot of the platform, Leyni let me walk on my own. I ascended the steps and stood opposite Kiev, my veil still covering my face.

Now that I was standing on the platform, I caught sight of Corrine, who sat in the front row next to Derek and Sofia. She had a huge grin on her face as she winked at me, nodding toward Kiev.

Ibrahim placed two gold rings in our hands and began the ceremony. I barely concentrated on what he was saying until it came time for our vows. Kiev reached for my hands, enveloping them in his.

"Mona," he began, his intense green eyes boring into me. "I never have been good with words. But I hope you'll believe me when I say that whatever love my heart is capable of, you have it all. If you'll accept me, I promise to be true to you every day for the rest of my life."

Tears began to brim in my eyes again. Kiev didn't realize how capable he was of love. Most men didn't possess half the heart he did, however many scars it bore.

"Kiev," I said, my voice trembling, "not long ago, I believed I would spend the rest of my life alone. Loveless, heartless. But you smashed into my world, breaking through my walls. For all I know of your scarred heart, I wouldn't want you any other way. You are my mirror. And if it weren't for your flaws, I wouldn't be deserving of you. You would be too good a man for me... The time I spent away from you was possibly the most painful of my existence. And I-I don't ever want to spend another day apart from you, my love. I accept you with all my heart... a-and I hope you'll accept me, too."

My voice choked up. Holding my hands gently in his, he slipped a ring over my finger. I did the same to him, and then he raised his hands to my face, lifting up my veil and tucking it behind my head. Ibrahim barely had a chance to give Kiev permission to "kiss the bride" before Kiev's lips were on mine as he kissed me passionately and pulled me against him.

A grin split my face through our kiss as Corrine wolf-whistled from her chair.

Showers of petals fell down upon us from the sky. Turning toward the crowd, I hurled my bouquet of flowers. There was a scuffle and Ashley emerged victorious. Perched upon Landis' shoulders, she clutched the bouquet triumphantly. A piano began to play to our left. I looked to see Rose sitting behind it. Three witches stood next to her, each holding a different instrument, and they began to accompany her. Kiev pulled me down the steps and we made our way to an open area on the beach Corrine had arranged as a dance floor. Other couples began to follow us. Resting my head against Kiev's chest, I closed my eyes, breathing in his musk, and lost myself in him. His lips pressed against my temple as we swayed slowly from side to side.

To anybody who didn't know us, Kiev and I were an unlikely couple. On paper, there was almost nothing we had in common. But beneath the surface, we had more in common than most couples could ever hope to have.

"What are you thinking?" he whispered into my ear, his voice husky.

"You're my lifeline, Kiev. You do realize that?" My voice was hoarse.

He held me closer. "And I won't let you down."

"Please don't," I whispered.

We passed the rest of the dance in silence, enjoying the music and the feel of our embrace.

"Mr. and Mrs. Novalic," Corrine called from the side of the dance floor. She was gesturing to a large cake on one of the food tables. She held up a knife. I smiled back at her and pulled Kiev over. Everyone stopped dancing and gathered round us. I took the knife from Corrine and positioned it over the cake. Kiev's hand over mine, we began to slice the cake together.

"Take the first bite," Corrine said as we placed the first slice on a plate. Kiev picked up a spoon and dug it into the sponge. He raised it to my mouth and fed me. It was a shame that he couldn't eat any of his own wedding cake. I could have sworn that I saw a look of disappointment in his eyes as he looked over the beautiful cake. Corrine sliced up the rest of the cake quickly using her magic and distributed it to everyone.

Picking up a plate of cake, I left Kiev's side and walked over to Rose. She was still playing the piano. I bent down, planting a kiss on her cheek.

"Thank you, Rose. You're an incredibly talented musician." I placed the plate on the seat next to her. "Why don't you take a break?"

"Thank you," she said, picking up the plate and standing up. She walked over to Caleb in the crowd and sat next to him.

When I arrived by Kiev's side again, he pointed to

the rest of the delicious-looking buffet laid out on the tables. "Won't you eat some?" he asked.

I shook my head. I slipped my hands beneath his suit, running them up along his back. I reached up to kiss his throat.

"I'm hungry for only one thing right now," I whispered.

I wanted nothing more than to be alone with my new husband. But people were beginning to dance again, as the witches kept the melody going. We decided to dance for another hour before finally retreating away from the crowds.

We'd almost reached the entrance to the woods when someone called out behind us. We turned around to see Matteo. I'd spotted him dancing with Helina just a moment ago, but now he walked toward us alone. He cleared his throat as he stopped in front of us.

"Kiev," he said, pausing and looking at him nervously. "I… I'm in love with your sister."

A flicker of surprise crossed Kiev's face, though I'd expected him to be more shocked. I'd seen the two of them dancing at the wedding today, but I hadn't known that they shared anything deeper than that. Not that long ago, Matteo had despised Kiev's siblings.

Matteo glanced back at the crowds. I followed his

gaze to see that it had fallen on Helina, who was standing in conversation with Erik.

"She doesn't know that I'm having this conversation with you," Matteo said, drawing his eyes back to Kiev. "But I want to marry her."

There wasn't even a moment's hesitation on Kiev's part.

"There isn't a man in this world I'd rather she ended up with," Kiev said, his eyes glistening as he nodded vigorously. Beneath my husband's joy, I couldn't miss the pain and guilt. Kiev had murdered Matteo's sister, Natalie. Now here was Matteo asking for permission to love and marry Kiev's sister, Helina.

A smile broke out on Matteo's face. He looked relieved.

"You didn't need to ask," Kiev said. "You know that I owe you more than I can ever repay."

Matteo looked once again at Helina. "Well… your sister will be a good start."

The two men embraced. Before Matteo headed off, he gave me a hug and kissed my cheek. "Congratulations, Mona. I wish you and Kiev a life of happiness."

I hugged him tight. Matteo had been like an older brother to me during some of the most painful and hopeless years of my life. "Thank you," I whispered.

Matteo left us and headed back toward Helina. Kiev watched him leave, positively beaming. "Well, that's one sibling sorted. Now there's just Erik…" He turned and looked down at me. "Now, where were we? Ah. Are you comfortable in that dress, my love? It looks rather tight. This ridiculous costume Corrine has put me in certainly is…"

Not willing to hang around for any more distractions, I gripped his hands and vanished us from the spot.

CHAPTER 6: CALEB

My eyes were mostly on Rose throughout the wedding. She looked more beautiful than ever in that light pink dress, her dark hair trailing down her back. As the hours passed by, and Kiev and Mona had left the beach, Rose continued playing along with the witches for those who were still dancing. I could see that her hands were growing weary. I walked over to her and sat down on the bench. Placing an arm around her, I whispered into her ear, "Shall I give you a break?"

She smiled, then shook her head. "I would rather play with you."

I acquiesced, although I would have much preferred

to see her resting. Planting my hands further up along the piano, I began to accompany her melody. As our harmony filled the air, the thoughts and emotions that I'd experienced during the wedding came back to me.

Watching the ceremony had moved me in ways I hadn't expected. With Rose sitting only a few feet away from the platform where Kiev and Mona had stood, I kept looking from them to her. My mind filled with images of Rose walking down that aisle toward me, the two of us standing on the platform, exchanging vows, sharing a kiss... I couldn't stop the scene from playing in my mind.

I wasn't sure why this wedding had brought about such a reaction. But it stirred something deep inside me. An ache. A desire. A longing to finally claim a woman as my own, to place a ring upon her finger, to both give myself and accept her completely... I thought back to the heat I'd seen in Rose's eyes the other evening. She'd wanted me to make love to her. I'd refused to that night. I hadn't even been sure why at the time.

But now I understood.

I looked back down at Rose expertly playing her piece, her brows furrowed in concentration, the flowers in her hair beginning to loosen and touch the sides of her face.

I wanted to commit everything I had to her before making her fully mine.

CHAPTER 7: ROSE

I was glad to be able to provide the music for the party. A wedding was just what this island needed. We'd been under so much stress, I could see how much everyone appreciated this relief.

People stayed on long after Kiev and Mona took their leave. They continued to dance and mingle even as sunset arrived beyond the island's boundary. Although my hands were aching, I didn't want to take more than a few minutes' pause. I was enjoying playing with Caleb too much. I hadn't played with him since I'd been trapped on his island as a prisoner.

I noticed Caleb looking at me a lot throughout the

wedding. I wasn't sure why he was staring at me. As we both took our third break, allowing Landis and Ashley to take a turn, I walked with Caleb toward the dance floor.

"You've been staring at me a lot today," I said, raising a brow.

Caleb smiled. "Then you must have been staring at me to notice."

I chuckled. "I guess so." I did find myself looking at him a lot. Partly because I still couldn't believe he was here with us on this island. It felt like a dream.

"You look stunning, Rose," he whispered into my ear as he led me to dance. "And I still can't quite believe you're mine."

I know the feeling.

As I draped my arms over his shoulders, his hands wrapped around my waist and he lifted me up suddenly so that my face was level with his, my feet hovering above the ground. He kissed my cheek and rested his chin on my shoulder, still holding me in the air. I giggled as my legs swayed.

Erik and Abby danced a few feet away. The way Erik was holding Abby close to him, and the way she nestled her head against his shoulder... I was surprised by how intimate they looked. I hadn't even known they were friends until recently. The attraction was unmistakable as they looked into each other's eyes.

When Abby caught my eye, I looked away again. Not wanting to make her feel uncomfortable, I turned my attention back to Caleb.

"How did you learn to play music?" I asked.

"Mostly, I just taught myself."

"Seriously?"

"I'm not sure why you're surprised. I've had a lot of downtime over the years."

"Did you ever go to school when you were younger?"

"Yes. The local town school, until the age of about thirteen. Then I joined my father's ship business as an apprentice architect and engineer… His dream had always been for me to take over running the family business."

He placed my feet back on the ground. I slipped my hand in his. Rather than returning to the piano again to relieve Ashley and Landis, I let Caleb lead me away from the dance floor, away from the lights and noise. We walked in silence and stopped again once we were far away enough for me to barely hear the music. I knelt down on the sand, pulling Caleb down with me. We lay on our backs, gazing up at the dark sky.

After a pause, I turned my head toward Caleb. "Does

this island feel any more like home to you now than when you first arrived?"

To my delight, he nodded. "It does... After the battle we just fought side by side, it would be hard not to feel camaraderie for the people of this island."

I reached out and brushed my fingers against his cheek before leaning forward to kiss his lips.

"You are part of this island," I said. "Part of this family. This place wouldn't feel complete without you now."

I held his hand and rested it over my navel before looking back up at the sky. I let out a sigh. I couldn't deny that this wedding had made me imagine what it would be like to one day wed Caleb. I could almost imagine him standing there at the head of the aisle, watching me as I walked toward him, my arm looped through my father's. It made me shiver.

I was about to lean forward and kiss him again when a wave of shouts broke through our peace. We sat up and looked back toward the crowd. The music had stopped, as had the dancing. Everyone was looking out toward the sea. I followed their gaze and gasped as I finally saw what they saw.

A horde of one hundred dragons, racing toward us in the distance. Although I knew they came in peace now, the sight of them still sent chills down my spine.

The dragons and their prince had returned.

Just in time to crash the party.

Chapter 8: Rose

The dragons were headed straight for the Port. Caleb and I lost no time in jumping to our feet and rushing towards the jetty to greet them. Others were less enthusiastic. They remained where they were on the beach, watching as the dragons drew closer and closer. My parents broke free from the crowd to join us.

The four of us stood at the edge of the jetty. My mother's grip tightened around my father's forearm. The dragons had crossed the boundary now—I could only assume that Mona had cast a spell upon Jeriad and his companions before they left, allowing them free entrance—and they were so close that I could begin to make out their features. I spotted the silver-orange scales of Jeriad, and the grey-blue body of Ridan. I also spotted several others who had accompanied them during the first visit. But right in the center of the crowd was a dragon larger than any I had seen before. He had piercing amber eyes, and his shimmering scales were pitch black laced with gold. I had thought that Jeriad was intimidating, but this magnificent creature made him pale in comparison. There was no doubt in my mind that this was the prince.

The horde soared over our heads and began to touch down in the clearing behind the port. Their landing was so deft and skillful, the ground barely shook. A strong wind built up around the area as their massive wings beat all around us.

The clearing was in no way large enough to hold all of the dragons, so as their feet hit the ground, they changed into their humanoid forms, making space for the others to land. Caleb, my parents and I walked slowly toward the clearing, and waited at the border until each of them had transformed. My eyes roamed the crowd of virile men in search of the prince. It didn't take me long to find him.

He was the most imposing and striking among them. With locks of thick dark hair that touched his sculpted shoulders, he retained his bright amber eyes. He wore a silken black cloth draped over his deep tan chest and his teeth were pearly white as he exchanged a word with Neros. Complete with a chiseled jawline, he looked like some kind of Grecian god.

My father looked down at me. "I suggest just the two of us approach first."

He held out a hand. I let go of Caleb and took it. We left him and my mother behind as my father and I began walking toward the dragons.

The prince stepped forward with Jeriad. As we approached within a few feet of them, my father and I stopped. Now that we were closer, I could see that the prince was almost exactly my father's height. The prince's eyes left my face and fixed on my father.

"Welcome," my father said, gripping his hand in a firm shake.

The prince nodded slowly.

"How do you like to be addressed?" my father asked.

"You can call me Theon," the prince replied, his voice deep and rumbling.

"This is Derek Novak," Jeriad said, "fire-wielder and king of this island." He gestured toward me. "And this is his daughter, Rose Novak, the maiden we had come to retrieve."

I couldn't hold the prince's gaze as he looked directly at me. I stared down at the ground. My father's grip around my hand tightened.

"Just so that there are no misunderstandings," my father said steadily, "my daughter is already engaged. But there are plenty of other worthy women on this island."

Engaged. It was strange hearing my father say the word. I supposed that it was a good idea to tell the dragons this. It would make my relationship with Caleb seem more fixed and unlikely to be swayed.

"So I have been told," Theon replied. "But it is a shame... I could have made your daughter very happy."

There was a tense silence, and even though I wasn't looking at him, I could practically feel his gaze blazing into me. My cheeks grew hot. Too hot for comfort. I was sure that they had turned a tomato-red color.

I was relieved when my father changed the subject. "Would you like a tour of the island, Theon? Or would you like us to take you straight to your accommodations?"

"There will be time for a tour later," Theon replied. "For now, my men and I would like to rest. It's been a trying journey."

"Of course." My father turned back to my mother

and Caleb, waiting a dozen feet behind us, and beckoned them over. I was relieved when Caleb walked to my side and placed an arm around me.

"Would they prefer to fly or walk?" my mother asked my father.

Jeriad overheard my mother's question and answered before my father could. "We'll walk. I know where the mountains are already. They're not far from here."

And so we set off through the woods. We walked the whole way in silence. I still couldn't get used to these men. Even when they were quiet, they exuded an intensity unlike any I'd ever experienced before. It was exhausting just being in their presence.

I was glad when we finally arrived in the clearing outside the Black Heights. My parents walked up ahead and pushed open the door to the inner chambers. I was curious to see what the witches had done with it. Caleb and I waited until all the dragons had entered before we followed them into the mountain. We walked along a winding lantern-lit tunnel in the direction of the storage chambers.

When we arrived in the first one, I gasped. It was totally unrecognizable. It had been fashioned into some kind of grand entrance hall.

Gone was the rough stone floor, and in its place was

luxurious black marble. The walls were covered with rich velvet drapes and a grand chandelier hung in the center of the room, casting soft light around the walls. The dragons' mutters of approval filled the chamber. From here, we exited through the door to our left and entered another tunnel, which soon widened into a broad hallway with carved rosewood doors on either side of us.

"The apartments along this hallway as well as the ones on the floor above us have been especially designed according to Jeriad's specifications," my mother said. "We hope you will find them to your liking."

The dragons began dispersing along the hallway.

"Theon," my father said, turning to the prince. "We were told that you had special requirements. Your quarters are along here." My father gestured to our left, toward a particularly large door right at the end of the corridor. We began walking toward it, and Jeriad followed. On reaching it, my father handed Theon the key. Theon opened the door and stepped inside. We followed inside after Jeriad entered behind the prince.

The beauty of the apartment took my breath away. The floors were the same black marble and although the furnishings were simple, they were elegantly done. Everything seemed to be designed to give the feeling of space. Although there were no windows, the high ceilings and minimal design of the place made it feel cool and airy, and all the furniture appeared to be crafted out of iron. We walked from room to room, admiring the job our witches had done and watching for Theon's reaction. So far he seemed satisfied. We stopped at the last room—the bedroom. The bed was huge, much larger than my parents' queen-sized bed, and the sheets and pillowcases were made of deep orange satin. Half a dozen cushions were piled up near the velvety headboard.

Theon turned to face us, a small smile on his face. He nodded courteously. "Thank you."

Still holding my hand tightly, Caleb motioned for us to follow my parents, who were backing away now. We reached the front door with Jeriad and were about to close it behind us when Theon spoke again. He was looking directly at Jeriad. "You may leave now, Jeriad. Get some rest. I will let our hosts know about tomorrow."

Jeriad nodded and backed away, strolling down the corridor to find his own quarters. We all turned to look back at the prince curiously.

"We don't want to waste any time in making acquaintance with the maidens on this island." Theon's amber eyes roamed toward me once again, making my skin tingle. "So if it's agreeable, we would like to arrange the introduction for tomorrow. Noon would be a convenient time for a ball. I trust you'll be able to manage this."

With that, he bowed slightly once again and closed the door, leaving us all standing and staring at each other in bemusement.

A ball?

I could tell from my parents' faces that they had no more clue what Theon meant by it than Caleb or I did.

"A ball," my father murmured.

"A ball," my mother repeated, frowning. "Rose, do you know what he means by this?"

"Oh, sure," I said. "I throw balls for dragon shifters every Friday."

Chapter 9: Rose

"A ball." I repeated the word again as we left the mountains. Since Theon had closed the door on us, my mother thought it best that we didn't knock for clarification. We looked around for the dragons who might still be strolling the corridors, but they had all retreated into their rooms and we didn't want to disturb them in case they were sleeping already.

So we were left to our own devices in figuring out what exactly Theon had meant.

"Come on," my mother said, a look of amusement on her face. "How hard can this be? They just want us to arrange for a formal introduction to all the interested ladies."

My father already looked fed up with the whole affair as he ran a hand through his hair. He looked at my mother, then at me. "Can I leave this ball business to the two of you?"

My mother chuckled, and nodded. "I think that would be best."

My father heaved a sigh. "Good. I have other, more pressing matters to see to now. I'll catch you around."

He left us and began making his way across the clearing toward the forest, leaving me, my mother and Caleb. I looked at my boyfriend. "Honestly, you're not going to find this interesting either," I said.

"Agreed," Caleb said, rolling his eyes.

My mother looked at Caleb, then back at my father who'd almost disappeared in the distance. "Hey, Derek!" she shouted across the lawn. My father spun around. "Take Caleb with you. He can help with whatever it is you need to do."

Caleb looked relieved to be let off the hook, and as he walked over to join him, the two men disappeared into the woods.

My mother turned back to me and held my hand. "I think it will be good for Caleb and your father to have some time alone, man to man."

"Great idea." I leaned forward and kissed her cheek. "And I'm happy to have some alone time with you, Mom."

She smiled and kissed me back. Then she let out a sigh. "So, the ball. Firstly, where do you suggest we hold it?"

I frowned, rubbing my face in my hands. "Well, when I think of balls, I think of Cinderella. The classic fairytales. They are all normally held in some kind of grand hall. I guess the closest we have to that is one of the chambers within the Black Heights themselves?"

"Hmm," she said. "Or we could ask Corrine to help us set up on the beach. We held a wedding there today, I don't see why it wouldn't be fit for a ball."

"Yeah," I said, "but it wouldn't really feel like a *ball*. It would feel more like a party, or something. I think we should hold it in the largest chamber we have in the mountains."

My mother smiled. "Okay. I trust your judgment more than mine, dragon girl."

We re-entered the mountains and took a sharp left turn. Eventually, after passing along several tunnels, we reached the chamber we'd had in mind. It was the largest that we were aware of. It was currently filled with sacks of grain and emergency supplies.

We stepped inside and looked around. "We'll need some help from the witches in making this place more… fairytale-ish," I said.

"Okay," my mother said. "Now we've decided on the venue, we need to think about music."

I began thinking over my music sheets and which pieces would be most suitable. But really, I wasn't worried about this. I wasn't lacking in knowledge of classical music, thanks to my father, and I was sure that this would be pleasing to the dragons. "Don't worry about music," I said. "I'll sort that out. What about food?"

"The dragons said that they would be satisfied with whatever the humans eat. So that shouldn't be difficult. We'll set out a buffet, something similar to what we had today at the wedding."

"Okay."

There was a pause as my mother and I looked at each other. It dawned on me—and I was sure on her too—that we'd both been avoiding the most important element of our ball.

The damsels themselves.

They still had no idea that I'd hooked them all up with these dragons.

"The single ladies," my mother said, reading my

mind.

"Yeah," I said, my mouth drying out.

My mother gulped. "Well, it's getting late now. I suggest we make a trip to the Vale early tomorrow and break the news to them then."

It would have to be *real* early if the ball was at noon. Many would want at least a few hours to get ready.

My stomach churned at the thought of none of them being interested. I had just assumed that dragon shifters would be appealing to them.

Now I just had to pray that this assumption was correct.

CHAPTER 10: DEREK

Caleb approached me across the clearing. Our eyes met, then we looked away and walked through the forest in silence. Even now, I still didn't find myself fully at ease in the young man's presence. I wasn't sure that I ever would. A small part of me resented my daughter staying with him in the mountain cabin. I wanted her at home. After all she'd been through, it had been heart-wrenching not having her sleep at home.

"Rose thanked you earlier for saving my life," Caleb said quietly. "But I haven't yet."

I shook my head. "Don't mention it."

Caleb had saved both my and Sofia's lives from

Annora's curse, going against his own people and risking his own life in the process. Saving him from Rhys was the least I could do.

We didn't talk again until we arrived back at my penthouse. I led him straight to my study. I had a hundred and one tasks going through my head that needed to be done, but now that Caleb was here with me, I wasn't sure that I wanted to do any of them. It dawned on me that, apart from Rose's recounting of everything that had happened to them since she'd been away from the island, I still knew very little about this young man. And that was something that I wanted to change.

"Take a seat," I said, gesturing to the chair opposite mine across the desk. "Do you drink?" I asked the question more out of interest than out of desire to give him alcohol.

Caleb shook his head. "Not anymore."

I raised a brow, pleased by his answer. "All right. Would you like some other refreshment?"

"Thanks, but I'm fine."

I sat down in my chair, folding my fingers together and resting them on the table, continuing to look steadily at him. "Since we have this time together, why don't you tell me your story, Caleb?"

Surprise played across the vampire's expression. "My story?"

"Yes. I still know very little about you, other than that we owe you our lives. I would like to know more... For example, how did you first become a vampire? What were you before you became one?"

Caleb's eyes darkened. "That's a long story," he said. "But if you have time, I'll tell it to you."

I glanced at the stack of papers on my desk, filled with notes and to-do items. I didn't really have time. But I would make time for Caleb.

As he began to recount his story, starting with his life as the son of a ship merchant, I found myself listening with rapt attention. His gaze was distant, and he seemed to drift off in some parts of the story, reliving his memories afresh. By the time he'd finished, hours had passed. I hadn't spoken once throughout, not even to ask a question. I was both deeply moved and also surprised by how much this vampire reminded me of myself during my darker times, before I met Sofia.

He paused after he finished, looking down at the table.

"You're a brave man."

Caleb scowled. "Not so brave. I allowed myself to live a life of hell for decades. If it hadn't been for Rose, I might even still be in that castle. In fact, I'm certain that I would be."

I understood what he meant. I remembered all too well what it felt like to be lost in the darkness. Darkness that was so easy to sink into as a vampire, yet so difficult to climb out of. If it hadn't been for Sofia, I was certain that I would also still be wallowing in it.

Perhaps Rose is to Caleb what Sofia is to me.

Caleb raised his gaze to my face, and whereas before his eyes had looked distant, now they looked focused. Almost fiery.

"Derek," he said. "I'm in love with your daughter."

I believed him when he said it. The sincerity and feeling in his voice was unmistakable.

I nodded slowly.

He wet his lower lip. "And when I feel the time is right," he continued, "I want to ask your permission to marry her."

My voice caught in my throat.

My girl, married.

The thought made me shudder.

It wouldn't be long now until she was eighteen, but she still felt like my little girl, despite how much she'd grown up.

I stood up and walked over to the window, steadying

my breathing as I looked out at the swaying trees. I could sense Caleb's tension as he waited for my answer. He got up from his chair and walked over to my side.

"I promise to protect her with my life. I pro—"

I held up a hand. Caleb had misunderstood the reason for my silence. It wasn't that I doubted him anymore. I just wasn't sure that I was ready to let my daughter go... to anyone.

I swallowed hard. Finally, I turned to face him, my mouth parched.

The earnestness in Caleb's eyes became my undoing.

Even though it killed me, I nodded.

I gripped his shoulders hard. A smile formed on my lips. "I don't think Rose would ever forgive me if I refused."

He breathed out sharply. I drew him in for a hug.

I remembered how hard it had been for me to win Aiden's trust and approval. As difficult as this was, I really didn't want to be as tough on Caleb. He'd been through enough hardship in his life for me to give him more when all he wanted to do was love and care for my daughter, just as I had for Sofia.

I took a step back, looking him over. "Achilles, eh? Rose Achilles." I crossed my arms over my chest. "Hm. Doesn't quite have the ring of Rose Novak... But it'll do."

CHAPTER 11: ROSE

I didn't sleep much that night. My mother invited me to stay the night in the apartment, but I preferred to go back to the cabin and wait for Caleb. I was already asleep by the time he climbed into bed. But I woke up again at about two in the morning, feeling his arms around me. I was happy that he'd gone to see my father. I would have given anything to listen in on their conversation.

"How did it go?" I asked, snuggling closer to him on the mattress.

He brushed his palm over my forehead. "Well," he said.

"What did you do?" I asked.

"I helped your father out in his study. He briefed me on a few of the many responsibilities he has on his shoulders."

"Did you find it interesting?" I asked.

"Very. A lot more thought goes into running this island than the one I used to live on... How did it go with you?"

I heaved a sigh. "Well, we figured out the venue, entertainment, and food. We just don't know if anyone will actually show up. My mother and I need to go to the Vale"—I looked up at the clock—"in a few hours, actually... in hopes of enticing some ladies to come and meet the dragons." I grimaced at the thought. I couldn't have made up a more bizarre situation if I'd tried.

"Then you should go back to sleep," Caleb said softly, still stroking my forehead.

Caleb was right. I needed more sleep. But as much as I tried, I couldn't. Caleb even managed to fall asleep before me. I lay awake well into the early morning hours. When I looked over at the clock again and it was four-thirty in the morning, I decided to get up. There was no point in wasting time lying down when so many things needed to be done before noon. I walked into the bathroom and brushed my teeth, then took a shower and got dressed. I checked in the bedroom to see that Caleb was still sleeping before scribbling a note and placing it at the foot of the bed.

Caleb, depending on when you see this, I'm either at my parents' house or in the Vale. I love you, Rose.

Then I left through the front door and began racing down the mountain. The crisp morning air was rejuvenating, the chirping of the birds filling my ears. I raced through the forest and didn't slow down until I arrived at the foot of my parents' tree. I ascended in the elevator and, to my surprise, saw that the kitchen and living room lights were on. Realizing that I'd forgotten my key, I looked through the kitchen window. My parents were both sitting at the dining table, deep in conversation. I rapped against the window. Their eyes shot toward the window and their expressions warmed on seeing me. My mother leapt up and rushed to the door to let me in.

"You couldn't sleep, Rose? Neither could I." She beckoned me inside and led me into the kitchen.

"Good morning, sweetheart," my father said, his voice sounding hoarser than usual. He took my hand and placed a kiss over the back of it.

"I've just been thinking about this stupid ball all morning." I looked at my mother. "Did you manage to speak to Corrine already?"

"Yes, I caught her before she left the beach last night. She's been working most of the night with Ibrahim and Shayla on the hall in the Black Heights. She said she wasn't tired anyway and was up for the challenge. Oh, and the witches will take care of the food, too. That's not a problem."

"Good." I breathed out. "I don't think we should arrive at the Vale any later than eight this morning."

"I agree. We could probably make that seven forty-five."

"In the meantime, I'm going to start gathering up my music and deciding what the agenda should be."

I got up from the table and walked through the penthouse toward the music room. I opened the cabinet in the corner of the room and began paging through my music sheets. Once I was happy with the assortment I'd pulled out, I placed all the sheets into a binder and tucked it under my arm. Then I headed back out of the room. As I neared the kitchen, I could make out my parents in conversation, but as I approached within earshot, they stopped talking. I couldn't help but wonder what they were talking about that they didn't want me to hear.

I walked back to the table and placed my music

down in front of my father. "Well, that's what I've chosen."

He opened up the binder and began paging through the sheets, nodding every so often in approval. "Good choice," he said.

My mother looked at me with concern. "We still have a few hours before we can leave for the Vale, honey," she said, "why don't you try to sleep?"

I shook my head. "I just can't. I already tried. I won't be able to sleep until this ball is over."

My father stood up, holding the music sheets in his hands. "Then why don't we give these a little practice?"

I leapt at his suggestion. "I'd love that."

We left my mother in the kitchen and headed back to the music room, both taking a seat on the bench in front of the piano.

He took out the first music sheet and placed it on the stand. I began to play. I managed to get through the entire piece without a single mistake, despite not having played this particular composition for at least a year.

When I'd finished, my father was beaming. "I still remember the first music lesson I gave you when you were six. It's hard to believe you're the same girl."

"Caleb's pretty awesome with instruments, too," I said, running my hands along the keys.

"Yes." My father smiled down at me. "I've heard him play." He cupped my face in his hands. As he stared down at me, I could have sworn that his eyes moistened slightly. "I'm proud of you, Rose. I'm so, so proud of you." He leaned down to plant a kiss on my head. "And I want you to know that… I approve of Caleb."

I raised a brow. "Really?"

His jaw tensed and even though he looked almost pained to admit it, he nodded, keeping his eye contact steady with me. "I'm not sure there's anyone in this world whom I could see as truly deserving of you… but Caleb's a good man. I can't deny that."

This was the first time that I'd heard my father outright approve of Caleb. He couldn't have known how much it meant to me. I flung my arms around his neck and buried my head against his chest. He pulled me onto his lap and cradled me like a baby.

"Thanks, Dad," I croaked.

We cuddled for a while longer, then I slipped back down onto the bench and continued to play the next piece. I played mostly solo, but for a couple of pieces, my father played an accompaniment.

The rest of the time passed quickly, and before I knew it, it was time for my mother and me to leave for the Vale. We bade goodbye to my father and entered the elevator. On reaching the ground, my mother offered to carry me on her back. Although I was taller than her, since she was a vampire, she was strong enough to carry me and run at the same time without problems. But I shook my head, realizing that she didn't know about my newfound speed.

"I can run fast now, perhaps as fast as you. Shall we race?"

My mother looked surprised, then grinned at me. "Let's go."

We began whipping through the trees and I was amazed that I could almost match her speed.

"I suppose I shouldn't be surprised," she said. "Your father never did lose his speed... I still wonder what caused this change in you though." She cast a sideways glance at me.

I shrugged. "It just happened soon after I saw Dad spouting fire."

"You'd never seen him do that before, had you? Perhaps it sparked something in your subconscious."

"Maybe... It's just strange."

We had already reached the Vale after barely a few minutes of conversation, so our voices trailed off as we prepared ourselves for what we were about to do. We reached the town square and stopped outside the bell tower. I looked at my mother, who was motioning to begin climbing it. I caught her arm and held her back.

"Mom, I should do this. I'm responsible for... this situation."

I didn't give my mother a chance to argue as I began climbing up the ladder. I reached the bell at the top, grabbed the rope and began swinging it wildly. My eardrums ached, as they always did when ringing this giant bell. But I didn't stop ringing until the square was filled with people. Some of them had clearly just climbed out of bed after a night of partying down on the beach.

I cast a brief glance down at my mother before clearing my throat. "Firstly," I began to yell down, "all of you who are not single ladies can go back to bed. I need as many single girls as possible gathered here in this square. If there's anyone you don't see here, please go and fetch them now."

I was met with a sea of confused faces, but I was relieved when they did as I'd requested. About half an hour later, the square was filled with I guessed just shy of a hundred and fifty women—a small fraction of those we had on the island, but they were enough for now. There were only a hundred dragons, after all.

Some of my classmates down below smirked and

waved at me. I smiled and waved down at them as I caught their eyes.

"So, ladies," I continued. "You are all single and looking?"

A couple of women shook their heads and shouted, "Not looking," but most were nodding.

To those who did shake their heads, I said, "Those who aren't interested in dating, please leave the square. This doesn't concern you."

The few who had shaken their heads left the square.

"Right," I muttered. Since most of the humans had not even witnessed the dragons firsthand—they had been inside the mountains throughout the battle and the dragons had all left soon after the battle had ended—I proceeded to explain the arrival of the dragons, my managing to win them over, and their reason for staying on the island.

Once I finished my story, I was met with stunned silence. My stomach dropped, and for one horrifying moment, I thought that nobody was going to step forward and volunteer.

Debbie, one of my classmates, broke the silence. "So you're pimping us out?"

"No!" my mother and I yelled at once, horrified at the thought. "If any of you don't find this appealing, you don't have to come. This is only for those who are interested in trying something… new."

To my relief, Debbie broke out laughing. "I was just pulling your leg, Rose."

I smiled back weakly. "So? Who wants to attend the ball at noon?"

A chorus of "Yes!" pierced through the morning air as every single woman standing in the square raised their hands. They hadn't even seen the shifters yet, but I supposed I must have done a good job at describing them…

"Okay," I said, after the screams had died down. "Then you should all aim to meet me in the clearing outside the Black Heights at eleven-thirty this morning. The ball starts at twelve, but I'd like you to arrive a bit early."

"Okay!"

I chuckled to myself as everyone dispersed. I climbed back down the ladder.

"Well handled," my mother said. "Now, I suggest that we go to the venue and see what the witches have done with it."

My jaw tensed. Although the girls' reaction had been a major weight off my shoulders, the main obstacle was still to come. We still had to pull off this ball and make sure it all went smoothly. Managing a hall filled with fiery dragons and vulnerable humans was a daunting prospect.

My mother rubbed my back. "Just a few more hours and this will be over."

CHAPTER 12: ROSE

I was relieved that all the girls arrived on time. *Well on time.* Two dozen arrived an hour early. My mother and I caught some wandering around the tunnels in search of the hall. We ushered them inside and asked them to wait in the corner until it was time.

The witches had outdone themselves again designing this place. The sacks of grain had been moved elsewhere and the rough floors had been smoothed into the same black marble that the dragons seemed to like. Several crystal chandeliers hung from the cavernous ceiling. A long table of food was already set out along one wall and we'd arranged cushioned seats all around the circumference of the hall. As an added touch, the witches had created a little veranda halfway up the wall and attached a winding set of stairs to it. This was to be the music balcony. The witches had placed a piano there and an assortment of other instruments I knew how to play. I'd also requested that two witches, Shayla and Leyni, stay with me and help keep the music going when I needed to take a break.

I looked at the watch on my mother's wrist. It wouldn't be long now.

"Why don't you go and bring in the others now? They should all be waiting outside."

"Good idea," I said. I could do with some fresh air. Although it wasn't particularly hot in the hall, all of these chambers felt claustrophobic to me. It was as though the dragons' heat emanated through the bowels of the mountain.

I hurried out of the hall, along the winding tunnels, and emerged in the clearing. Sure enough, all the other girls were waiting for me. They all had looks of excitement and apprehension on their faces. I noted how much care they'd taken in their appearance. Their hair was done up beautifully and they all wore gowns and high-heeled shoes. As I walked toward them, I was again struck by how weird the situation was. Like a fairytale. Cinderella with dragons. *All we need now is a pumpkin.*

I looked down at my own clothes. I was just wearing pants and a sweatshirt. I would keep myself on top of the balcony anyway, so hopefully my attire wouldn't offend anyone. Debbie and a few other classmates hurried toward me in the crowd.

"Have they arrived yet?" Debbie asked.

"No," I replied. "We're not expecting them before noon."

I led everyone down the tunnels and back toward the hall. My mother greeted us at the entrance, inviting everyone to take a seat. My classmates wanted to sit and talk with me more, but my nerves wouldn't allow it. I wasn't able to sit still. I stood up and wandered over to the buffet. I walked along the assortment of steaming stainless-steel vessels. I called my mother over.

"When it comes time to eat, we'll have actual tables, right?" I asked. "So it will be like a proper banquet."

"Don't worry," my mother said. "Corrine thought of that. At around one o'clock, after everyone's had a chance to introduce themselves, the witches will arrange for a long table and help with the serving."

"Good."

I almost leapt out of my skin when there was a

thundering knock at the door. The girls began chattering excitedly, but as my mother reached the door, a hushed silence fell about the hall. My mother opened the door to find the first dragon standing behind it. Jeriad. He looked freshly showered and more radiant than ever before. He was dressed in simple yet luxurious clothing—light linen pants and a loosely fitted shirt that exposed a generous amount of his toned chest. As the other dragons began entering after him, they all looked similarly dressed.

I was surprised that the prince hadn't been the first to enter. But I didn't stay to watch. I wanted to make it up to the balcony before he arrived so that I wouldn't have to meet him again.

I scrambled up the stairs and didn't look back down at the floor again until I'd reached the top. Now that it was noon, the witches were beginning to arrive to help out—Shayla, Leyni, and a couple of other witches, though Corrine wasn't among them. I guessed that she was finally having a well-deserved sleep.

As I peered over the railing, I kept my head down low, just so that I could see, but wasn't easily seen. To my surprise, Theon was the last to walk through the door. He wore a deep blue cloth draped over one bulging shoulder that perfectly complemented his tan skin. Approaching the center of the room, he stood next to the other dragons. They had all gathered together and were looking casually around the room at the ladies in their seats. I couldn't spot a single girl in the room whose cheeks hadn't already flushed.

My mother approached the shifters and greeted the prince. He bowed courteously, taking her hand and placing a chaste kiss over the back of it. They exchanged a few words, and then my mother backed away. She looked in my direction and gave me the thumbs up. I glanced back down once more toward the dragons, and to my surprise, Theon's amber eyes were fixed directly on me. I backed away quickly and sat down behind the piano. I didn't like the way he was looking at me... as though I was some sort of challenge.

He'd better keep his artistry of romance to himself.

If he tried anything with me, I would tell him in no uncertain terms which direction to head in. So I hoped that he would heed my father's warning and leave me alone. Heck, we couldn't afford to offend these dragons. The safety of our island depended on them now. Hopefully the prince was a gentleman.

Placing my fingers on the keys, I began to play. A few moments later, Shayla appeared a few feet away from me and picked up a clarinet. She positioned herself behind me, so that she could view my music sheet as I played, and began to accompany me.

From where I sat, I could still make out what was going on through the holes in the balcony. The dragons had begun to disperse, and were making their way toward the *damsels* seated around the room.

As they reached each girl, they bowed their heads slightly and held out a hand. The girls accepted, and I was sure at least a few of them were close to hyperventilating as the shifters placed their wide palms around their waists and began leading them to a slow dance. Their forms were so imposing, they dwarfed even the tallest of women.

Not a single word was exchanged as the dragons looked intensely into their partners' eyes—as though just looking at them was conversation enough. Most of the girls looked too tongue-tied to speak even if they'd wanted to.

My eyes wandered around the room toward Jeriad. He had made a beeline toward my blonde friend Sylvia, who looked ecstatic.

For the next fifteen minutes, they continued to take in their companion's every detail. Once Shayla and I paused for a few moments to mark a change of pace, they planted gentle kisses upon their women's hands and moved on to a new partner, where more gazing ensued.

It appeared that the dragons had no desire for conversation at all. At least, not yet.

It's like these men are trying to see through to the very souls of these girls.

Perhaps they did possess some kind of deep intuition and could judge a person from their eyes. Somehow, I wouldn't have been surprised. Their gazes were so piercing.

I continued to look around the room, and once again Theon surprised me. He was standing at the edge of the hall, and he was showing no signs of approaching anyone. He wasn't looking at me now—he was just watching his fellow shifters dancing. Several of the girls who were still seated were casting glances at him. Of course, they would sooner faint than approach him.

Why is he standing all alone? Jeriad had said that primarily, they had come here to find a partner for the prince.

I didn't understand his behavior, although my suspicion left me ill at ease. I looked over at Shayla and nodded toward the prince.

"Why do you think he's just standing there?" I whispered.

She shrugged. Although from the look in her eye, she

had the same suspicion as me.

I stopped staring down below and focused on my music again. I didn't know how long this ball would last. None of us did. I supposed the dragons would make it clear once they felt that they'd had a satisfactory introduction.

Hopefully not more than a few hours.

I kept my concentration mostly on my music for the next hour, though I couldn't help but keep glancing down every now and then. The dragons maintained that silent demeanor throughout, just staring at their partners, as though nothing else existed in the world except the girl in front of them. I felt goosebumps run along my skin just thinking about attempting to hold their gaze for more than a few minutes, let alone hours. But almost an hour had passed now, and the girls seemed quite happy to be lost in their eyes.

I was relieved once one o'clock struck and Corrine arrived. She appeared near the food table and began talking with my mother, who cast a glance up at me and nodded. That meant it was time to start wrapping up the music.

Shayla and I finished the piece gracefully. Then, standing up, I caught sight of Theon again, still standing at the corner of the room. He hadn't danced with a single person the whole hour, nor had he made any attempts to. I was surprised that even Jeriad hadn't tried to pair him up. I could only assume that he'd requested to be left alone.

I remained watching from the balcony as Corrine manifested a long banquet table. Gripping their partners by the waist, the shifters led them toward the edges of the hall as the witch floated the table into the center and lined up chairs around it with her magic. She spread out a pearly white tablecloth, followed by piles of silver plates and cutlery.

"Please take a seat," she announced.

The shifters approached the table with the girls, pulling back chairs for them to take a seat first, before sitting beside them. I was glad to see Theon seating himself at the head of the table. A part of me kept expecting him to climb up to my balcony.

The witches began to serve the feast deftly with their magic, placing all of the vessels in the center of the table and serving everyone. I could barely remember when I had last eaten, but I had no appetite now. Even though the food looked delicious, I shook my head when my mother beckoned me over.

"Later," I mouthed.

My mother shook her head. "Now," she mouthed

back.

I sighed and obeyed her, climbing down the steps. I took the plate she had prepared for me before hurrying back up to the balcony to eat. As soon as I'd taken the first bite, I was glad that she'd insisted. Having food in my stomach eased my nerves.

Shayla ascended the stairs toward me, holding a plate in her hand, and sat down next to me to eat.

"So do you know what's going to happen now?" I asked.

"Your mom said that she spoke to Jeriad. Apparently that's all the dancing that will be done today."

I widened my eyes. "But Theon hasn't even danced with anyone yet."

Shayla shrugged, brushing aside a strand of her brown hair as she began to eat. "It seems that one hour of dancing was enough for this introductory ball. Apparently, all the dragons who danced have chosen a lady each, and now the second stage is to whisk them away somewhere on the island to talk in private, without distractions."

"Oh… And then after that?"

"I don't know," the witch replied. "I don't think Jeriad explained the next step to your mom…"

I stayed up on the balcony with Shayla for the next

hour or so. We both finished our meals and then sat on the bench by the piano, watching as the dragons and their partners finished theirs. Soon, the shifters began helping their ladies out of their chairs and leading them across the hall toward the exit.

I stood up and walked to the railing for a better view. Surprisingly, Theon seemed to have left already. Perhaps he'd left early. I was still puzzled by his behavior.

Well, that was over much sooner than I thought.

This more than suited me though. Now that the stress of the ball was over, I found my exhaustion returning—the plate of food I'd just eaten likely contributing to it.

I bade goodbye to Shayla and made my way down the steps. My mother was standing by the table talking to Corrine. Putting an arm around me, she planted a kiss on my forehead. "How are you feeling?"

"Sleepy," I muttered.

"Go to bed now," my mother replied. "It seems our work here is done."

I gave Corrine a hug. "Thanks for helping with this."

"No problem."

I waited for all the ball attendees to exit the hall before leaving my mother and following after them. I wandered down the tunnel toward the main exit, brushing my hands along the rough walls. It felt like a huge weight had been lifted from my shoulders. I had almost reached the last stretch of tunnel before the main exit when a deep baritone voice came from behind me.

"Princess."

The dragon prince stepped out of the shadows.

"Theon," I gasped.

He stopped a couple of feet away from me, his amber eyes boring into mine.

"Do you mind if I ask you a question?"

"O-okay."

"Who do you believe is the most worthy maiden?"

His question took me by surprise. "Most worthy maiden," I began. "Hm. That's really a tough question. There are, uh, so many worthy maidens."

His thick eyebrows furrowed as he scrutinized my face.

"Why aren't you mingling with any of them to just see for yourself?" I asked.

A smile curled the corner of his lips. "I don't... mingle as freely as my comrades do."

"What do you mean?"

"I mean I don't just dance or talk with anyone."

I frowned. "Then I'm not sure how you will ever find

yourself a partner. If you don't—"

"My comrades are now seeing the worth of each of the maidens before suggesting whom I ought to grant a private meeting to. I just thought that, in the meantime, I would ask you for your opinion."

Oh.

A wave of relief washed over me.

"Well, as I said, that's a tough question for me to answer. I think you're better off just waiting for your comrades' feedback on the girls."

"Very well," he said, stepping away. "I'm sorry to have held you up."

"T-that's quite all right."

I was taken aback by his courteous behavior. It left me feeling almost guilty for expecting him to try something with me. As he turned around and began walking back down the corridor, toward his apartment, I realized that perhaps he truly was a gentleman. I hadn't detected him trying to lure me in. Although his very presence was intimidating, he had acted anything but dishonorably.

As I left the Black Heights and began racing back toward Caleb's and my mountain cabin, I couldn't help but feel happy for the girl who would eventually end up with him. He would make her very happy indeed.

CHAPTER 13: SOFIA

Soon after Rose left the hall, I left too. I was feeling as exhausted as Rose had looked. I hurried back to our apartment and headed straight to the bedroom. I stripped and changed into my most comfortable pair of pajamas before seeking out Derek. He was in his study, as I had expected he might be. He looked up as I entered, leaning back in his chair and stretching out.

"How did it go?" he asked.

"Much smoother than Rose and I could have expected." I walked over to him and sat down on his lap. I ran a hand through his hair, placing a kiss on his cheek. "I'm so proud of our daughter."

Derek's face filled with melancholy—an emotion I'd grown used to seeing in him since Caleb had told him he wanted to propose to our daughter. Derek just didn't want to let his baby go. Neither did I, but I couldn't deny that I was thrilled. I trusted Caleb and I knew that he would rather die than see anything happen to our daughter. He was also more grounded and mature than Rose in many ways, and I saw that they complemented each other.

Derek would get used to it. I knew he would. I held his hands and stood up, pulling him up with me.

"You look tired. Come to bed with me?"

He didn't resist as I tugged him out of his study, back toward our bedroom. I collapsed on the bed almost as soon as we entered and crawled between the sheets. Derek took a shower before settling on the mattress next to me. He lay on his back and stared up at the ceiling.

"At least Caleb seems a much safer vampire to be around than I was for you."

"I would have to agree with you there," I said, grinning. I squeezed his warm cheek, turning his head to face me. "Speaking of vampires, how long are you going to wait before turning back?"

"I'm not sure. I want to wait a while to see how

things play out."

We fell into silence, snuggling closer to each other and staring into each other's eyes until exhaustion eventually claimed me and I fell asleep.

***

Derek and I were woken unceremoniously a few hours later by a frantic knocking on our bedroom door. Derek leapt out of bed and swung the door open.

My heart sank as soon as I saw that it was Eli.

"Eli? What is it? How did you even get in here?" Derek asked.

"You left the front door unlocked," Eli said. "There's something on the news you need to see."

I shot out of bed, rushing to Derek's side. I clutched Eli's shoulders. "Don't tell me this is about Ben again."

Eli shook his head. "Definitely not Ben."

I could breathe somewhat more easily, although his expression didn't give me reason to feel much relief. Since Eli's TV was the only one on the island that had been hooked up to all the news channels, Derek and I hurried directly out the front door. As we raced through the forest toward Eli's penthouse, I couldn't help but feel sad that I was beginning to associate Eli's visits to us with fear and dread.

We reached Eli's tree and hurried up the elevator. As he pushed open the front door, I was shocked at how messy the living room was. Eli wasn't always the most tidy of people, but this level of disorder… it was worthy of a teenage boy's room.

I shoved the thought aside as Eli switched on the television.

"I should've noticed this earlier," he muttered, flicking through the channels. "I just haven't checked on the news for couple of days. Been feeling a bit under the weather."

My mouth fell open as he stopped changing the channels.

"More CCTV footage," Eli said, pointing with the remote toward the scene playing out on the screen. A dozen or so hooded figures dressed in black, wielding a burning ring of fire, closing in on hundreds of young men and women.

"Rhys," I gasped. "Who else could this be but the black witches?" I clasped a hand over my mouth, gaping at the screen. "Oh, no. No. Why are they doing this?"

"The code of secrecy has already been broken," Derek said. "They are no longer bothering to hide themselves from humans."

"But why do they want all these teens?" I stammered.

"Why are they so bent on capturing people?"

Derek shook his head slowly. "I don't know." He looked at Eli. "We need to call a council meeting this instant. Wake everyone up. I want Caleb there too."

CHAPTER 14: DEREK

Sofia and I sat at the head of the table in the Great Dome. We watched as our council members piled in, bleary-eyed and confused, and took seats around us. I didn't answer any questions until everyone had arrived—everyone except Yuri and Claudia, who had already left the island for their honeymoon. Xavier took a seat next to me, Vivienne next to Sofia.

Caleb was the last to enter—without Rose, I was glad to see. He took a seat at the opposite end of the table after closing the main door behind him.

"What happened, Derek?" Ashley asked, wiping sleep away from her eyes.

"The black witches have moved on to new shores."

Mona's mouth fell open.

"Where?" she asked.

"They closed in on a group of adolescents at a school, near the coast of California. The police are reporting just over a hundred missing. The black witches cast a spell and vanished them. It was all caught on camera. This is just the first attack of God knows how many." I looked around at my comrades. "They must be stopped. And if we don't do it, nobody will."

"But how?" Zinnia said, her face deathly pale.

I looked toward Mona. "You know more about these black witches than any of us."

Mona chewed on her lower lip, looking around the room. "I don't know exactly what all this blood is for—"

"Blood?" Sofia interrupted, horror in her eyes.

Mona raised a brow. "Yes, blood. What else would they be taking these humans for? I don't know exactly what they need them for, but it's for some kind of ritual. I suspect this has to do with Lilith, the one Ancient who remains clinging to life by a thread. Whatever this ritual is, we need to stop it."

"This Lilith seems to be the cause of most of our problems," Kiev muttered. "We need to end the bitch."

Mona scoffed. "Easier said than done. I don't even

know where she resides. I've visited her island before with Rhys, but he made sure I didn't know the actual location."

I looked toward Caleb. "You know, don't you? You and Rose were on that island."

"I have no idea where it is within the supernatural realm, but we do know that there is a gate leading to it deep in the Amazon jungle."

"Do you remember exactly where the gate is?" I asked. "Could you locate it in the jungle?"

Caleb looked doubtful. "That night we arrived there, I was so bent on getting as far away from that gate with Rose as I could, I'm honestly not sure if I could remember its location now. I could try, but God knows how long it would take me to find it again. The nearest city is Manaus, but that hardly helps us."

Mona shook her head. "I can't believe that Rhys would've allowed that gate to remain open if you and Rose had escaped through it. Even if you manage to find the location, I'm sure he would have closed it. Lilith is far too precious to them."

"I don't understand the logic of going after Lilith," Gavin said. "Maybe I'm just missing something, but surely we would have to end all of the black witches?"

"I doubt they'd be left with much steam if they lost

Lilith," Mona said. "They want to take over The Sanctuary and revive the lost way of the Ancients. They want to reinstate black magic that today's witches have mostly shunned. Much of the power that they have, they gained from Lilith. If we managed to take her down, I don't know if they would be successful without her. They might even lose some of their powers. Heck, I might too. Most of the power I possess came as a result of a meeting with Lilith."

"And while we are contemplating this impossible task," Sofia said, "more people could be being abducted as we speak."

"Mona," I said, "you really believe that Lilith is the key here?"

Mona nodded slowly. "I just don't know how we could—"

"If you can't figure out how to end her, then nobody will be able to. Please, go now and take some time. Think back to all those years you spent with the black witches. Think back to your meeting with Lilith. Try to figure it out. The rest of us wouldn't even know where to start."

Mona's eyes fell on her husband as she gulped. Then she nodded, and although there was no confidence in her expression, that nod alone gave me some hope. She stood up from her chair and left the Great Dome.

I looked now at Sofia, her forehead creased with worry.

"In the meantime," I continued, "we must try to prevent more kidnappings. It's impossible to know exactly where they will strike next. But I think we can all be confident that they will strike again. And they will not travel far when they can find what they need nearby. It seems they are targeting younger people. We need to make it more difficult for these witches to get access to them." I paused, steeling myself for what I was about to say. "We need to do what we have never done before in the history of this island. We need to make contact with the police."

"What?" a chorus of voices gasped.

"We need to make contact with the police," I repeated steadily, "of all our neighboring shorelines, and call for a closing of schools. Children and teenagers alike should be kept inside and people should avoid going out. Each household should be equipped with guns, with instructions of what to do if a black witch shows up—"

"Gun or not, a human family wouldn't stand a chance in hell if a witch showed up in their living room," Landis said.

"I'm not saying they would," I replied. "None of these measures will stop them. We can only attempt to slow them down. You all heard what Mona said. These witches are on a blood hunt unlike any before. We can't let them perform whatever ritual they're trying for. Because if it's successful, I suspect that the white witches of The Sanctuary will only be the first among many to feel their wrath…"

Ashley looked at me, disbelieving. "What, so we're just going to show up randomly at a police department and tell them that all the schools need to be closed? Why would they even listen to us in the first place? What if they ask for ID? What if they ask where we're from—?"

"There is no need to reveal The Shade, and there is no need to reveal our identity. After this violent introduction to the existence of supernaturals, not only by the black witches but also by Ben, I believe that they will be open to talking with us. I suggest that a human and a vampire go." I looked at Sofia and she nodded, as if reading my mind. She stood up next to me, placing her hand over mine on the table. "My wife and I will go. We will also need a witch so that we can travel quickly." My eyes rested on Corrine, who nodded. Next I turned to Xavier and Vivienne. "My sister and brother-in-law will take over ruling the island during our absence. You have the dragons here now helping to protect us. While we're gone, I don't think anyone needs to be worried about our safety. It's the world around us that is in jeopardy now."

Chapter 15: Sofia

We had no time to lose. Neither Derek, Corrine nor I knew how long this was going to take. Hopefully, if the humans weren't too difficult to convince, we wouldn't be gone more than a day.

We decided to head to the place where the first abduction had taken place in California. After the meeting was adjourned, Derek and I hurried back to our apartment to get ready for the journey, while Corrine returned to the Sanctuary to make her own preparations.

We hoped that by the time we returned, Mona would have formulated a plan on how to get rid of

Lilith once and for all. In the meantime, we had to do what we could to prevent more human lives being lost.

We hurried about in our bedroom, stripping out of our pajamas and changing into comfortable and durable clothing. I pulled out a large umbrella from one of the cupboards and tucked it beneath my arm.

It was still early in the morning and we had no desire to wake Rose up. We would be back soon and Caleb would inform her of where we'd gone.

"Are you ready?" Derek asked.

"Yeah. I think so."

We left the bedroom and made our way toward the living room to find my father standing there. He looked at us with concern. He drew me into a hug and kissed my cheeks.

"Be careful," he said. He squeezed Derek's shoulder before stepping back from both of us.

We descended to the forest ground and parted ways. Derek and I headed straight for the Sanctuary to pick up Corrine. We found her standing on her doorstep, lost in a passionate embrace with her husband. We waited until they were done before approaching. Corrine left her husband's side and came to stand next to us. She had a map in one hand, and a thick cloak was wrapped around her shoulders. She breathed out heavily. "Okay, let's go."

She held onto both of us, and the peaceful courtyard of the Sanctuary vanished.

When we stopped spinning through the air and my feet touched solid ground, my vision came into focus. We were standing outside a large rectangular building, lit by fluorescent lighting. After adjusting my clothes, I ran my hands through Derek's hair, smoothing it out. Then we headed straight for the entrance.

A plump, baldheaded man was sitting behind a wide wooden desk in the entrance area. He looked up as we entered. Surprise showed in his eyes. We had tried to wear clothes as plain as possible, but I supposed we still looked odd to him with our rather old-fashioned cloaks, especially me with my pale skin, and at this early hour of the morning.

He stood up, all five foot of him. "What can I help you with?"

"We have some information that will be of interest to you," Derek said.

"Regarding what?"

"The school incident."

The man's eyes widened. "Please take a seat," he said, gesturing to the seats around his desk.

We did as he'd requested, watching as he picked up a

phone and dialed a number.

"Three people are here regarding the incident at the school," he murmured, looking over us once more. "Can you see them now? Okay."

He put the phone down and beckoned us over again. Retrieving a ring of keys from one of the drawers in his desk, he got up and pushed open the narrow door directly behind him. "Alex," he called inside.

A young man appeared in the doorway wearing a uniform.

"Take these people straight to Wilson's office," the bald man said. "He's stayed late."

Alex nodded and led us out of the room toward a flight of stairs. We climbed two levels up before stopping outside a door labeled twenty. He knocked.

"Come in," a deep voice called.

Alex pushed the door open. We stepped inside and found ourselves in a small office, lit by bright strip lights. A tall man stood behind a narrow desk. He had grey-streaked hair and deep lines in his forehead.

The police officer held out a hand for each of us to shake. "Officer Wilson. Your names?"

Derek replied before Corrine or I could. "My name is Kyle Ardene. This is my wife, Claudia Ardene, and this is our friend, Ashley Novalic."

I would have fought back a laugh at the mishmash of names Derek came up with had my stomach not been in knots. Corrine scowled discreetly.

The man's gaze fixed on Derek. "Mr. Ardene, what can you tell me?"

"There will be another attack. Likely more than one. Schools need to be closed. Adults and children alike need to stay in their homes. Each household must be equipped with at least one gun."

Before Derek could continue, Wilson held up a hand. He reached into a drawer and pulled out a camera and a mini-tripod.

"I'm going to record this, if that's okay." He set up the tripod so that the camera was pointed toward the three of us and pressed record. Then Wilson folded his hands on the table and leaned forward in his chair, watching Derek intently. "Please repeat what you just said."

Derek acquiesced.

"How do you know this?" Wilson asked. A deep frown settled in on his face.

"By now you may have realized that there exist beings who are very different from you. Nonhuman, supernatural beings. The three of us are such beings. That's how we know."

Wilson's frown deepened. He looked from Derek, to me, to Corrine, then back to Derek again.

After almost a minute's pause, he said, "What exactly do you mean by… supernaturals?"

"The type the world has already seen in the news. Vampires. Witches…" Derek placed an arm around me. "My wife here is a vampire." He caught my eye and nodded. I raised my lips and bared my fangs.

"Dear God," Wilson whispered, gaping at me in disbelief.

"And Ms. Novalic here," Derek said, gesturing toward Corrine, "is a witch."

With a flick of a finger, she levitated a pen on the man's desk into the air and made it do a twirl before setting it back down again. The man's mouth opened and closed like a fish's. He looked at the three of us as though he still couldn't believe his eyes.

"And you?" Wilson said hoarsely, addressing Derek.

"My powers are not safe to display in this room."

Wilson stood up, his legs shaking. "W-wait here, please. I need to make a phone call."

We watched the man leave his office and walk into the adjacent room. I heard him pick up a phone and begin talking to someone—a superior of his, by the sound of it.

"That was really the first surname that entered your head for me?" Corrine muttered.

Derek ignored her, his eyes fixed on the door.

Wilson returned about twenty minutes later.

"I have spoken with my superiors and called for an urgent meeting."

"Your superiors need to issue a warning nationwide," Derek said, standing up. "And they need to do it as soon as possible."

"When and where do you believe that they will strike again?"

"It's impossible to say exactly when, but I'm certain that it will be soon. As to where, we don't know. Hence, you must not delay in this."

"Those black hooded people in the schoolyard footage, you say they are… witches?" Wilson asked, still looking as though he was in a daze.

"Yes. The worst kind," Derek said, looking straight into the camera as though addressing Wilson's superiors directly. "The best chance of surviving an attack by them is to shoot them through the palms. That's where their powers emanate from."

"And y-you three. Where have you come from?"

"That's not important. Just understand that not all supernaturals seek to prey on humans. We are here because we want to help you." Derek turned once more to the camera, his eyes boring into it. "You *must* heed our advice."

"Mr. Ardene, you must come with me to headquarters. My superiors will have many more questions for you. We would like to conduct an extensive—"

Derek shook his head, cutting him off. "Perhaps in the future, but we don't have time for that now. We just came to deliver this warning." Derek held out a hand, gripping Wilson's so firmly Wilson winced slightly. "I trust your superiors will make the right decision and do what is needed. Goodbye, Officer."

Before Wilson could say another word, Derek looked toward Corrine and nodded. She held both of us by the hand and the brightly lit office disappeared.

When we reappeared again, it was on a beach.

"We're still in California?" I asked Corrine.

The witch nodded. I looked up and down the empty shoreline, the sun still hours from rising above the horizon. I caught sight of the promenade behind the beach, lined with beautiful houses, not unlike Derek's and my dream house that we'd spent the first five years of our twins' lives in. I was overcome by a bout of nostalgia. The life we'd lived in that house seemed so distant now, like a past life. I swallowed hard, forcing my thoughts back to the task at hand.

"So we're just going to assume that Wilson's superiors will take care of things?" I asked.

Derek nodded. "We'll have to. We did our part. Wilson filmed the meeting. He has proof of our display of powers, so there's no way that his superiors can think he was hallucinating. After two displays of supernatural existence broadcast on mainstream media, we have to hope that his authorities will be more open-minded than to completely reject what we had to say."

"And now," I said, "what about South America? The countries lining the Pacific Ocean also aren't far from the witches' base."

"We'll start trying to meet with authorities in Mexico and make our way down along the coast," Derek replied. "But we simply don't have time to visit all of them. We'll go as far as Panama. Hopefully our warning will start spreading to other countries." Derek must have caught the doubtful expression on my face. "Sofia, I know this is a pathetic situation. We just have to try to do what we can."

"What if the witches start moving to other parts of the world for easier targets?" I asked.

Derek heaved a sigh, casting a worried glance out

toward the horizon. "We have to hope that Mona will find a solution before it comes to that."

Chapter 16: Sofia

The South American authorities proved to be harder to get through to, mostly because of the language. A lot of the lower officials didn't speak English and Corrine's knowledge of Spanish was rusty, as was mine. We certainly weren't anywhere near as fluent as my twins.

The process took us longer, but eventually we managed to reach an authority along the coast of each country who could grant us a reception. By the time we reached Panama, the sun was almost setting. I was glad to have remembered my umbrella. I'd had to use it a lot throughout the day.

The heat was suffocating as we arrived outside the

police department in Panama City. My mouth was parched and my skin felt rough and dry. My body just wasn't used to this type of heat. We entered through the main doors into a small entrance area, and then took a right through a door into a reception room. I groaned internally at the sight of huge windows letting the evening sun stream through into the room. It was crowded in here, and I didn't want to risk opening up my umbrella in case I ended up poking someone in the eye. Rather than disturb Corrine and ask her to put a spell on me to shield me from the sun, it was easier for me to step outside while Derek and the witch waited in line to be seen.

I made my way back into the small entrance area. It was much darker here with fewer people. I leaned back against the wall, relishing its coolness, and took deep breaths. I closed my eyes, resting my stinging eyelids. Although I'd been careful to keep the sun from shining directly onto me, the brightness still affected me.

A beeping opposite me broke through my moment of peace. It sounded like it was coming from the pocket of the fair-haired man standing opposite me with his head buried in a newspaper. He cast a brief glance my way, then folded away his paper and walked toward the exit. I leaned my head back against the wall again, closing my eyes and trying to find a moment of peace again.

I rested for a few minutes before Corrine poked her head through the reception room doors and called me over. The three of us walked with an official into the back offices and we repeated much the same process as we had with Wilson with the dark-haired, mustached police officer we sat in front of here. He spoke better English than most of the others we had seen in South America, which helped things move along.

Once we had shocked him enough to agree to film us and pass on our message to his superiors, we left. Since he didn't try to insist that we stay, Corrine didn't need to vanish us. We walked back to the entrance hall, where I pulled out my umbrella and opened it. The sun had almost set now and the light was much softer as we stepped outside.

"So," Corrine said, "we'll go home now?"

"I'm up for that. Derek?" I looked to my husband.

His eyes were fixed on a spot on the pavement on the other side of the road. His eyes widened. "Sofia, duck!"

Before I could register what was happening, Derek knocked me off my feet and a smash behind us filled my ears. Shards of glass rained down upon Derek and me. As I tried to sit up, he forced me back against the ground.

Winded, I gasped, "Derek, what—?"

Corrine had ducked beside us now too, her face marred with confusion.

"Corrine," Derek said hurriedly, "that cluster of trees further up the beach. You see it? Take Sofia there and wait for me. If anyone approaches, vanish her further up the beach."

"What—" I choked.

"A man across the street just tried to shoot you, Sofia," he hissed. "A man I'm sure is a hunter."

Chapter 17: Derek

I wanted nothing more than to scorch that man to ashes. The fire burning in my fingertips was begging for release. But I had to reel in my temper. I had to see the bigger picture.

As soon as Corrine vanished with my wife, I threw myself against the car nearest to me and peered over the roof. I caught sight of the man's blond head hurrying away down the pavement. I wasn't going to let him get away. Ignoring the commotion behind me that was forming at a bullet having just been shot through the window of the police department, I raced across the road and began chasing the man.

He looked over his shoulder and stopped as he saw me. He didn't raise his gun again as I had expected him to, perhaps because I was clearly not a vampire.

I closed the distance between us quickly and grabbed him by the collar. I pulled him away from the pavement and took a right down a narrow cobbled street filled with market stalls and teeming with people. Wrestling the gun out of his hands, and checking him for any other weapons he might have been carrying, I pulled him through the crowds. I stopped at the other end of the street where there were fewer people and hauled him down a narrow alleyway. I slammed him against the wall, pinning him there by his shoulders.

"Who are you?" I hissed as he struggled beneath my grip. "You're a hunter?"

He nodded, scowling at me. "Who the hell are you?"

"Derek Novak."

His jaw dropped. "Novak?" he croaked.

"That will be the last word you utter if you don't listen to me," I whispered, digging my fingertips into his flesh. He winced as I applied heat.

"What are you?" he whispered.

"Human. Hunter. Vampire. Fire-wielder. I have, and have had, many titles. But none of them define who I am." I shook him. "Do you understand me?"

He cried out as a surge of heat passed through my fingertips and seeped into his flesh. Sweat dripped from his forehead.

"You almost killed a person who was trying to accomplish the very thing that you spend your days fighting for," I snarled. I picked him up and slammed him against the opposite wall. "Not all supernaturals are the same, just as not all humans are the same. There are evil and good among all races." I bashed his head against the wall again. "Get that into your thick skull before you go shooting at an innocent person again."

"What are you doing here?" he gasped.

"We have just spent all day traveling through countries trying to protect the lives of humans," I said through gritted teeth. "Something you almost killed my wife for doing."

He looked shaken enough by now, his face drained of all color, so I let go of him, though not without first jolting him with another wave of heat.

He staggered back further down the alleyway, stopping and staring at me.

"My family and my people are your allies, not your enemies," I said, trying to calm the storm raging within me. "The black witches are the ones you need to focus your energy on ending. They are the root of all this trouble now."

"Black witches," he breathed, "they are the ones who stole those teenagers from the school?"

I nodded grimly.

He frowned. "But some vampires are still our enemies. You forget about the incident in Chile. It was caught on camera, a vampire tearing through innocents' throats. Do you know the vampire who did that?"

My voice caught in my throat. The hairs at the back of my neck stood on end. Clenching my jaw, I shook my head.

"I don't know that vampire." I breathed out heavily. "But what I'm saying is that the black witches are the primary threat now. They are the ones we need to be focusing on. So just... don't just go shooting at any vampire you see, all right? Especially if you suspect that they are one of my people."

The hunter nodded. I stepped aside, handing him his gun back, before he raced away.

"I don't know that vampire."

The words echoed around in my head long after the hunter had disappeared. It pierced my heart to realize that it was true.

The man I'd seen in that footage was not my son.

At least, not the son I knew.

CHAPTER 18: BEN

The Oasis. Once the home of the Maslens.

I stared around at the lavish atrium, barely believing what Jeramiah had just told me. My parents had told me about this place, the history it held. My mother had been imprisoned here by Borys Maslen. It was also where Benjamin Hudson had lost his life, as well as my uncle, Lucas Novak. The Oasis held a lot of meaning for my family. None of it good.

I was already unsure about the decision I'd made to join Jeramiah's clan. Now the situation just seemed even more inauspicious. I glanced at Jeramiah, who seemed to be watching my reaction closely. I did my best to conceal my shock.

"You have a very impressive place here," I said.

Jeramiah smiled. "Shall I give you a tour?"

"Sure," I said, my mouth dry.

Jeramiah began leading me forward along the ground level that encompassed the beautiful gardens in the center of the atrium. Most of the doors we passed by were closed, but Jeramiah pushed the occasional one open to reveal luxuriously furnished chambers and apartments. They were all decorated similarly—opulent Egyptian furniture, shiny marble flooring, bright murals on the walls, warm, soothing lighting. A few of the doors Jeramiah pushed open were dark and I could hear snoring coming from them.

"Most of these scoundrels are sleeping now," Jeramiah said. Letting down his dark shoulder-length hair, he shook it out before gathering it up above his head and tying it back in a bun. "You'll get to meet them soon enough."

"How did you find this place?" I asked.

"This place is legendary. Most vampires know of it. It had been thoroughly destroyed by the hunters when they destroyed the Maslens' coven. But since then, we've managed to not only rebuild it but also reinstate security. We have a number of witches living here with us. Hunters still know about this place, but they can't get inside."

Having walked full circle, Jeramiah gestured toward the glass elevator.

"You've seen this lower level now, more or less," he said. "Of course there are the human chambers. They're down in the basement."

"Where do you keep your half-bloods?" I asked.

"Most of them live among us. Those who serve us stay in servant quarters built into our apartments."

"What about the man I just half-turned, Tobias?"

"Oh, yes. I put him down with the humans for now until he stabilizes a little. Then we'll decide where to put him up..." Jeramiah frowned at me. "I haven't offered you any blood since we arrived. Would you like some?"

I ran my tongue over my lower lip. Truthfully, I could really do with some blood. I nodded. "Please."

"In that case, let me take you straight to my apartment—my refrigerator is fully stocked. You can explore the other levels another time. They're mostly just filled with apartments and halls similar to what you've seen on the lower level anyway."

We ascended in the elevator up to the highest level and stepped out. I followed him forward. He stopped after we passed the fifth door. Withdrawing a key from his pocket, he slid it into the keyhole and the door clicked open. It was dark inside. He flicked a switch and the lavish apartment lit up.

"Jeramiah?" a groggy female voice called.

Jeramiah smirked. "That's my half-blood, Marilyn," he muttered. Raising his voice, he called, "Hey, baby."

He led me toward a door at the end of the hallway that was ajar. He pushed it open to reveal a huge, dimly lit bedroom. A blonde girl lay stretched out on the bed, apparently naked but for a sheet wrapped around her. I backtracked into the hallway, leaving Jeramiah and his girl alone.

"So you brought Joseph back with you?" she asked.

"Yeah," Jeramiah replied.

She appeared in the doorway, still wearing nothing but a thin white sheet, Jeramiah standing behind her. She was pretty with large brown eyes and pale, freckled skin. She gazed up at me, squinting in the light.

"You'll have to excuse my girlfriend," Jeramiah said, sliding his hands around her waist and kissing her shoulder. "Marilyn can't be expected to look presentable at this time of day."

"Hi, Joseph," she said, winking at me. "Nice to meet you." Her eyes roamed my body as if she were undressing me in her mind.

Apparently noticing, Jeramiah gripped the back of her head and pulled it down as he planted a forceful kiss on her lips. "Watch where your eyes wander," he said.

He rolled his eyes at me before leading me away from the bedroom. I caught Marilyn still eyeing me from the doorway as we walked away. Jeramiah took me into a large kitchen. There was a beautifully carved rosewood table in the center. Stored in cabinets above the sink were silver cutlery and a number of crystal glasses.

The vampire strolled over to the tall fridge in the corner. When he opened it, it was filled with shelf upon shelf of jugs filled with blood, except for the bottom level, which appeared to have some human food—Marilyn's, I assumed. He pulled out two large glasses from one of the cabinets and set them down on the table. He filled them up with blood and handed one to me. I eyed the glass, sniffing it before taking the first sip.

The cool liquid glided down my throat like sweet ecstasy, lighting up my taste buds. This was the most delicious blood I had tasted since turning into a vampire.

Jeramiah was watching my reaction with mild amusement. He raised his dark brows. "Good?"

"Yeah. Really good. Where do you get this blood?"

Jeramiah flashed a smile. "Let's save some surprises for later, shall we?"

He began drinking from his glass, draining it in seven gulps. He poured another glass for himself, then topped mine up. I stopped after three glasses. I could have consumed more, but I was still holding out hope that I might be able to wean myself off human blood and replace it with animal blood. So while I was here I wanted to accept only what was absolutely necessary for me to not feel hungry.

"Shall I take you to your room now?" Jeramiah asked. "You look like you could do with some rest."

I gave him a faint smile. I doubted I'd be able to sleep, but I was eager to be alone. "Yeah, I'm pretty exhausted."

Jeramiah stood up and placed the blood back in the fridge. He gestured casually to the glasses. "My servant will clean those up."

"Marilyn is your servant?" I couldn't help but ask.

"No, no. She's my girlfriend. There's another half-blood living in the rooms at the back of my apartment."

Truth be told, I was surprised that Jeramiah had made a girlfriend out of the half-blood. I had just expected them all to be used as servants. It made me feel at least a little better about this place, that not all half-bloods were enslaved.

We exited Jeramiah's apartment, stepping back onto the open veranda connecting all the apartments. He pointed to a door on the same level, on the opposite side of the atrium.

"We lost a member of our coven recently," he said. "He used to live over there. You can have his place now."

"What happened to him?" I asked.

"He tempted fate. Got drunk out of his mind one night, ended up leaving our base and wandering around outside in the desert... You see, our witches have secured this place from the hunters. But the protective boundary only stretches so far around The Oasis. This vampire was foolish enough to step outside of it. Hunters are notorious for having people positioned around this area. Our coven has annoyed them too many times for them to give us an easy ride anymore. So let that be a lesson to you. Don't go more than five miles from this place if you want to avoid being burned from the inside by a hunter's bullet."

"Thanks for the tip," I said grimly.

We arrived outside the door to the apartment. It wasn't locked, so Jeramiah pushed it right open. He switched on the lights to reveal an apartment very much like his own. He took me on a short tour, showing me the master bedroom, two smaller bedrooms, three bathrooms, a large kitchen, a sitting room, servant quarters right at the back, and to my surprise a sauna—at least, it looked like a sauna.

He noticed my confusion as I looked at the wooden room.

"Yes, this is what it looks like. A sauna. Just a basic courtesy for the half-bloods living among us. Since they are not fully vampires and only display partial symptoms, being cold all the time can become uncomfortable. Saunas help to ease some of the discomfort."

"I see. Well, I won't need any half-bloods in my quarters," I said.

Jeramiah gave me an odd look, holding my gaze for a moment, before shrugging. "As you wish… I'll leave you now. Have a good rest."

I saw him to the door and closed it as he left. I leaned back against the wall, taking in the atmosphere of the apartment. There was a subtle aroma of sandalwood in the air—incense perhaps. I walked into the master bedroom. One entire wall was taken up by the mural of an exotic-looking beach. I smiled bitterly. It reminded me of my mother's Sun Room. *How far away I am from there now…*

I headed into the en suite bathroom, turning on the golden taps and relishing the cool water. I raised my head and stared at myself in the mirror. My eyes weren't pitch black as they had been, but they were still a much darker shade of green than usual. Hopefully, if I was able to abstain from killing, they would return to their usual lighter color.

Jeramiah was right about me looking like I needed rest. Still, I had no desire to even try sleeping. I stripped out of my soiled clothes and stepped into the shower. The water gushed down onto my back, soothing me like a massage. I still couldn't get over the facilities of this place. How lush it felt. I never would've dreamed in a million years that we were in the middle of the desert. They certainly wouldn't have been able to do any of this without the witches. I wondered how they had gotten them on their side to begin with and how many were here altogether. I had only seen one so far—Amaya.

I reached for one of the soft white towels hanging on the rack and dried myself. Wrapping the towel around my waist, I headed back into the bedroom. Opening one of the cupboards, I found a pile of clean cotton pants and shirts. I pulled one of each off the shelf and dressed, then sat down on the bed directly opposite the mural. I stared at it, my vision unfocused.

I just have to keep my head down and wait this out. At least I won't cause any more harm to anyone while staying here.

Chapter 19: Ben

I passed the next several hours lying on my back, staring up at the ceiling.

I replayed everything that had happened since I had left The Shade over and over in my mind, trying to make sense of my behavior—why I couldn't have just transformed like every other vampire in The Shade.

It was a relief that at least I was able to think straight. Those hours I had spent in the submarine, submerged in darkness, had been one of the most terrifying experiences of my life. It had been like being on a trip I'd feared I would never come down from.

It had been a while now since I had killed someone. I

could only assume that my theory was correct—blood in itself didn't bring about that extreme reaction in me. It was the actual killing, giving into my urge to claim life. To consume. To devour.

I wondered what was going on in The Shade now, whether Rose had returned, and what was happening with the black witches. Whatever the island was going through, I knew that my parents and my people were better off without me. I would only be adding risk to an already treacherous situation.

I still didn't know exactly what Jeramiah wanted me for. He had said that I would be useful in half-turning humans. I would have to explain to him that the only way I could half-turn a human was if he or she was sick. There was no way I would agree to touch a healthy one. I didn't trust myself to not kill the human in an instant.

Yet I wasn't sure that half-turning humans was truly why Jeramiah had shown interest in me. Michael, Jeramiah's comrade whom I'd met back in Chile when I'd first come across them, had said that if they needed newly turned vampires to create half-bloods, they could just create a new vampire themselves. Besides, I wouldn't be newly turned for long. A fair amount of time had already passed.

But whatever Jeramiah's true intentions were, there

was no point in reading too much into them now. I just had to watch my back and keep to myself as much as possible. Hopefully I would feel in a fit state to return to The Shade sooner rather than later.

***

As midnight approached, there was a knock on my door. Opening it, I found Jeramiah standing on my doorstep. He held a glass of wine in one hand. He was shirtless and wore dark pants, similar to the ones I was wearing. I noticed the tattoo of a black cross etched into his right bicep.

"I hope you weren't sleeping?" he asked, a slight slur to his voice.

"No."

"Good. I wanted to introduce you to some of the others. They are awake now."

The last thing I felt like doing was going down to meet a crowd of people, but I couldn't just refuse. They were letting me stay here. I had to put at least some effort into being sociable.

"Sure," I said.

I followed him out the door. We walked along the open veranda toward the glass elevator.

"We're out in the open tonight," he said.

We ascended one level in the elevator and stepped out onto the glass-walled platform that overlooked the entire atrium. I looked up to see that the trap doors in the ceiling were wide open, the light of the moon streaming in. As we climbed the stairs toward the exit, the temperature became warmer, although as we stepped onto the sand it wasn't as hot as I had expected. There was a cool desert breeze.

Looking around, I was surprised at how many men and women I saw—vampires, half-bloods and a few whom I guessed were witches. Exotic music filled the air from a corner where four women sat playing stringed instruments I didn't recognize and a tambourine. To their left was a long table filled with containers of blood and alcoholic beverages. Men and women were dancing, and scattered loosely around the dance area were large cushioned chairs. Dozens of vampires shot glances toward Jeramiah and me as we began making our way toward the drinks table. Five men and women—half-bloods—stood behind it, serving drinks.

"What do you want?" Jeramiah asked me.

"Nothing, thanks."

"Oh, come on. You need something to hold in your hand."

"A small glass of blood then," I said. "But don't add

alcohol. I don't drink."

Jeramiah faced the young woman looking tentatively at us from behind the table. "You heard him." He turned to me. "Why don't you go and take a seat over there." He gestured toward an empty chair. "I'll top up my drink and bring yours over."

I nodded, crossing the sand and sitting down. I noticed Michael—the blond vampire I'd met with Jeramiah back in Chile. Michael Gallow, if I remembered correctly. He looked at me coldly, holding my gaze for but a moment before averting his eyes to the girl sitting next to him.

Jeramiah arrived and handed me my drink. He took a seat next to me and reached for Marilyn, who was sitting on a cushion nearby, pulling her by the arm to sit on his lap.

"Well, this is Joseph," he said. "Joseph Brunson."

The crowd looked at me curiously.

"Hello," I said.

There was an awkward silence as Jeramiah started a side conversation with Marilyn. My eyes roamed the vampires, witches and half-bloods surrounding me. Counting those on the dance floor and those seated, there seemed to be at least a hundred. And there might still be more down below in the atrium. I couldn't help but notice the same black cross Jeramiah had tattooed on each of their arms—even the witches'.

"Why don't you dance for us, Marilyn?" Jeramiah said. Marilyn threw him a sultry glance before standing up. She slipped off the sheer coverall she was wearing to reveal a two-part outfit that showed her pale stomach. She raised her hands above her head and began to dance among those seated in chairs, weaving in and out.

Jeramiah watched her, a contented expression on his face, before addressing me again. "I'm sure you're wondering where we have all come from, and how we found this place."

"I am," I replied, taking a small sip from my glass of blood.

"Well," he said, "I suppose the story starts when I was still a human. A young man. Eighteen years old. I'd already lost both of my parents and, finding nothing better to do with myself once I hit my late teens, I decided to travel East. Whatever few possessions I owned I packed up and set off. It was a long, long journey, but I enjoyed the distraction. I traveled from country to country and ended up in North India. I stayed in the foothills of the Himalayas for several months. I loved it there."

"Yeah, and he's kept the long hair ever since," the

black-haired witch, Amaya, interrupted with a smirk.

Jeramiah rolled his eyes at her before continuing. "India was also where I first encountered a vampire. I was out for a walk late one evening. A vampire pounced on me and infected me with his venom. Hours later, I woke up as one myself. The same vampire who turned me ended up bringing me to a coven situated deep within the Himalayas. I spent the next God knows how many decades there. I lost track of time—one day just rolled into the next. But it was in that coven that I met everyone you see here today—except for our half-bloods, of course. They were created by us later."

"Your witches belonged to that coven, too?" I asked.

Jeramiah nodded, looking toward Amaya again. "We have six witches in total. They'd been staying within the coven. Amaya and I used to be lovers."

"Firmly in the past," Amaya muttered.

"Anyway," Jeramiah continued. "Twenty-odd years ago came the fall of the Elders. They were locked out of Earth and we were free to leave. Nobody was sure where we would go, though. But none of us vampires felt like staying where we were. It was a small place and it held too many memories we wanted to forget. I had heard about The Oasis. I'd heard of the Maslens' demise. I led everyone who wanted to follow me here. With the help of our witches, we managed to salvage the place and make it inhabitable. It was a slow process to get The Oasis to what it is today."

"I can imagine," I said.

Jeramiah's eyes glazed over as they fixed on the sky. He ran a finger slowly around the edge of his wine glass. "Life is good here," he said. "No hassles. No responsibilities. We live like kings and do what we want, when we want. I'm sure you won't want to leave."

I nodded stiffly.

"So why don't you tell us your story?" Jeramiah said.

I drank again from my glass, buying myself some time as I thought about what I should say. "Well, as I mentioned, I was taken in by the black witches. I stayed on the island that was governed by Caleb Achilles. I imagine my story is pretty typical amongst most vampires. I stumbled upon a bloodsucker one night and then got pulled into this crazy world. I haven't been turned long, so there's not much more to tell."

Jeramiah watched me intensely. It looked like they all wanted to hear more from me, but I wasn't going to offer it. The less said, the better.

I took another sip, and as I did, a light feeling began

to form in my head. I looked down at the blood, wondering if it had been accidentally, or perhaps purposefully, laced with something. I placed the glass down on the ground and stared at Jeramiah.

"What exactly did you bring me here for?"

Everyone else looked curious to hear Jeramiah's answer—except for Michael, who was now engrossed in conversation with the girl next to him.

"Well, it's not often we come across a rogue vampire. Especially not a newly turned one. You had nowhere to go. We have room for you. I didn't see a reason not to take you in."

I was about to inform him about my inability to half-turn healthy humans, but I held my tongue. I would wait until he actually asked me to turn one before informing him of this. There was no point before then—for all I knew, the occasion might not even arise.

Jeramiah placed his now empty glass down on the sand and stood up. He walked over to where Marilyn was dancing. Catching her hands, he placed them around his neck and slid his hands down to her hips. He led her toward the main dance area.

I took that as my cue to leave. At least for now, Jeramiah appeared to have had enough conversation.

And my head was feeling lighter and lighter. I couldn't be sure if it really was something in the drink. Perhaps it was something about this desert air making me react like this. Whatever the case, I stood up.

"Excuse me," I said. "I'm not feeling my best at the moment."

Most of the crowd nodded understandingly. Jeramiah called to me as I passed him. "Leaving so soon? The party hasn't even started yet."

"Yeah," I called back. "I haven't managed to sleep since I got here. I'm going to try now." To my surprise, a yawn escaped my mouth as I finished the sentence.

"Catch you later," Jeramiah said.

I entered the trap door and climbed back down onto the platform overlooking the atrium. Descending in the elevator to my floor, I headed straight for my apartment. I locked the door behind me, my feet now strangely heavy. *What is wrong with me?*

Dropping down on the bed and closing my eyes, I fell asleep almost as soon as my head hit the pillow.

When I woke up several hours later, it was to a burning feeling in my right bicep. My head pounding, I sat upright and looked down at it:

A black cross etched into my skin.

It seemed that whether I wanted to become a member of this coven or not, I'd just been marked.

Chapter 20: Rose

I woke the next morning to find myself alone in bed. I sat up, rubbing my eyes and looking around the room.

"Caleb?"

I slid out of bed and exited the room. He wasn't in the bathroom, or in the living room. I caught sight of him standing outside on the veranda, leaning against the railing and staring out toward the ocean.

I opened the front door and joined him outside. I walked up behind him, wrapping my arms around his waist and burying my head against his back. His hands closed around my arms, holding me against him.

"Something has happened, Rose," he said quietly.

He turned around to face me, looking down at me with a serious expression on his face.

"What?"

"The black witches. They're now on a rampage like never before. They're stealing masses of human teenagers."

My breath hitched. "What? How do you know?"

"They've been caught on camera. Your father called a meeting in the Great Dome last night and requested that I was present."

"Oh, my."

"The first victims we know of were a group of adolescents in a schoolyard. Your parents have left the island with Corrine. They've gone to try to warn the humans on the neighboring shores. In the meantime, Mona is trying to figure out if there's any way we can end Lilith. Mona believes that she is the key to our problems."

My mind was still fixed on my parents. "But how would warning humans do any good? Even with the warning, there would be no stopping those black witches."

"Correct. But we need to make this as difficult for the witches as possible. We need to delay them in this ritual they are trying to carry out."

"So they are meeting with the police?"

Caleb nodded.

"When will they be back?"

He shrugged. "We don't know. Your parents hoped they would be able to return within a matter of days."

My head was beginning to reel. So much had happened since I had fallen asleep several hours ago.

Frustration filled me that my parents had left without me. I didn't want to just sit here on this island. I wanted to help do something to combat this situation.

Caleb seemed to notice my restlessness. He frowned as he looked down at me. "What are you thinking?"

"I hate sitting still." I began pacing slowly up and down the floorboards. "Has Mona made any progress since they left?"

"I've heard no news."

Caleb's words replayed in my mind.

We need to make this as difficult for the witches as possible.

More difficult...

"My parents have left, but is everyone else still here?" I asked.

"To my knowledge," he replied.

There were so many more of us on this island, just sitting here. It seemed a waste of time for us to just be sitting here doing nothing.

I sat down on the bench, dropping my head into my hands as I racked my brain.

Think, Rose. Think.

Caleb crouched down in front of me, placing his hands either side of me on the bench. "Your parents wanted us to stay put until they returned."

But we didn't know when they were returning.

As I looked up into Caleb's eyes, an idea struck me. Now that I'd thought of it, I wondered why it hadn't occurred to me immediately.

Placing my hands on Caleb's shoulders, I stood up. "Wait here for me. I'll be back soon."

Chapter 21: Rose

I left Caleb on the veranda and began hurrying down the mountainside. I ran so fast I almost tripped up a few times, but I didn't slow down until I reached the entrance to the Black Heights.

The doors had been left wide open. I ran inside and began hurrying along the tunnels toward the dragons' residences.

I could feel my body temperature rising—sweat forming on my brow—as it always seemed to do when I was in these creatures' proximity. I had already reached the first corridor where the dragons' apartments were when I remembered that I was still wearing my nightgown. I had been too immersed in thought to pay any mind to my appearance. I straightened out the nightgown as best as I could and combed my hair with my fingers, trying to make myself look at least a little more presentable before approaching the nearest door to me and knocking.

Hopefully I'm not disturbing anyone too early. I had no idea who was residing in this particular apartment. When the door opened, I found myself face to face with Ridan. His brown hair was tousled and he wore nothing but a sheet wrapped around his muscled waist.

I took a step back. "I'm sorry. I hope I didn't disturb you."

He shook his head dismissively.

"I won't keep you," I continued quickly. "I just wondered if you could tell me where Jeriad is staying?"

Ridan poked his head out of the door and looked toward his left. He pointed down the corridor. "Jeriad's door is right at the end."

"Thank you."

I hurried off and Ridan closed the door behind him.

I placed my ear against the wooden door as I arrived outside, listening before knocking. To my surprise, I could hear the strumming of some kind of string instrument emanating through the wood, giving me confidence.

I rapped against the door. The music stopped and footsteps approached.

The door swung open and Jeriad appeared behind it. He was fully dressed—at least, as dressed as these dragons ever seemed to get. His chest was still bare but he wore long dark pants and a deep green cloth wrapped around his shoulders. He raised his eyebrows in surprise on seeing me.

"What brings you here, maiden? Would you like to step inside?"

I shook my head. "That won't be necessary. First, I wanted to ask you how it went last night with the, uh, damsels."

A subtle look of contentment settled in on the dragon's face. He nodded slightly. "This island is blessed with some beautiful females."

"Did you manage to… single anyone out for the prince yet?"

"Not yet. We have arranged for another meeting with the maidens tonight, when each of us will talk further in confidence. After that, we should have come to a decision."

"Ah, I see."

It dawned on me that I hadn't asked the girls how

their dates had gone. I made a mental note to do that as soon as I could. I guessed, however, that most of them had gone well if the dragons were meeting them again tonight.

"I wonder," I continued, dragging my focus back to the real purpose of my visit, "would it be the end of the world if you postponed those meetings to tomorrow evening?"

The dragon frowned. "Why would we do that?"

"Well, it might not be necessary, but I wanted to ask you for a favor. I wanted to ask if you would be able to accompany us on a trip. We would leave this morning and hopefully return by the afternoon, but... I don't know exactly how it will go. It's possible we won't be back until tonight."

"Where do you want to go? And how many of us would you want to accompany you?"

"At least fifty would be good. Honestly, we can't have too many. As to where, it is somewhere not too far from here. Within the human realm."

He crossed his arms over his chest, breathing out deeply. "I suppose that our prince won't mind a day's delay. Now that I think of it, it might be beneficial to have a short break between the meetings. It will give both parties more time to mull over our first meeting."

"Thank you. I do need to speak to someone else before finalizing details. I will return in less than an hour. Would you be able to let the other dragons know in the meantime?"

He nodded, his aquamarine eyes boring into me. I felt them roam my nightgown, then settle back on my face.

"Thanks again." I curtsied and turned on my heel. Hurrying away, I heard the enchanting melody strum up again as I exited the hall.

***

Now I had to speak to Mona. I hurried across the clearing and into the woods. I still wasn't used to the speed at which I could travel now. It only took me ten minutes to reach Mona and Kiev's tree, whereas previously it would've taken at least an hour—and that would be if I'd been jogging.

As I ascended in the elevator, I found the witch pacing up and down on the balcony, one hand wrapped around her midriff as the other rested against her temple. She seemed to be completely oblivious to me, even as I neared within a few feet of her. I had to call her name.

"What is it?" She raised her gaze to me. She looked

irritated at being disturbed.

"Caleb told me everything," I said. "And I have a request to make of you. I know you've got a lot on your shoulders right now, and I would much rather do this without you, but there's just no way we can—"

"Rose, please just get to the point."

"I want to ransack the witches' islands. Both the island that Caleb used to rule and Stellan's island."

Mona's eyes widened. Before she could object, I continued. "Do you think there's any possibility that those humans they kidnapped could be on their island?"

"It's possible, I suppose," she said slowly. "But Rose, this type of mission is extremely dangerous. You'd be marching right into their own territory. Things might have changed since you last visited. You don't know what you might find there now."

"But we have dragons. I already spoke to Jeriad and he agreed to let us bring at least fifty of them with us."

Mona still looked doubtful. "I don't think you should do anything until your parents return."

I sighed impatiently. "But we don't know when they will return. Isn't time of the essence? In the meantime, we could be doing something to help. I know you need to stay here and think, and you don't have to help us storm the place. We just need you to assist us in breaking through the first island's boundary so we can enter. Once we're finished there, we'll try to take one of their vampires hostage so we can enter the second island."

She fingered the ends of her hair. "And if you come face to face with Rhys? Have you thought about that?"

"It's possible that the black witches aren't even there. They could be on another kidnapping excursion. And if they are, well, many of them will be injured anyway from the battle here in The Shade. And those who aren't injured… we'll just have to be careful."

Mona bit her lip. "Your parents may never forgive me for allowing you to go through with this," she muttered. "But… all right. I'll help you break through the first island's boundary, and then you'll have to handle things from there."

Kiev entered the balcony, apparently having overheard our conversation. He walked toward me, eyeing me closely. "You have guts, girl." Then he turned to face Mona. "I will accompany her."

I could see pain in the witch's eyes. The last thing she wanted was for her husband to go riding off into an attack with us, but she seemed to know better than to argue with Kiev when he was bent on something.

"Kiev, could you two start gathering some others to

come with us? Since we have so many dragons, I don't think it's necessary for more than a handful to come," I said, as a plan began to form in my mind. "In fact, having more could be a disadvantage."

"Very well," Kiev said.

"I'm going to get Caleb now," I said. "I suggest we bring at least one werewolf, and we should also bring a witch, aside from Mona, who won't be staying with us long—perhaps Ibrahim—and then the rest could be vampires. It doesn't matter as long as they are not humans."

The couple nodded and we hurried down the tree, parting ways as we reached the ground.

It's time to give those witches a taste of their own medicine...

CHAPTER 22: CALEB

Rose. She had become a whirlwind. Whenever there was talk of danger, her first instinct wasn't to recoil, like most sane people. No, the first—and only—thing she thought to do was walk right into it.

Her courage was a gift, but I also feared that it would become her downfall. I couldn't help but feel she was beginning to spin out of control.

As I sat on the steps of our cabin, waiting for her to return and explain to me whatever wild idea she'd just gotten into her head, I found myself wishing that just once, she would allow herself to rest. I had come close to losing her too many times of late. I just wanted to lock her up.

I stood up as I caught sight of her emerging from the woods at the foot of the mountain and climbing up toward me. Arriving at the cabin, she gripped my hand and pulled me inside.

"Let me talk to you while I take a shower," she said. "We don't have a lot of time."

I entered the bathroom with her, waiting patiently at the door as she removed her clothes. I tensed as I laid eyes on her bare form. Her soft curves and smooth skin still made the predator within me stir, even now. I leaned back against the wall, watching as she began to soap herself down.

"I spoke to the dragons," she said. "And I spoke to Mona. I think we should storm the black witches' islands and try to retrieve the humans they've stolen."

Truth be told, I had already expected this, so her words didn't come as much of a surprise. I eyed her steadily as she looked toward me for a reaction.

"So?" she said. "What do you think?"

There was no denying it. I would relish every second of scorching the island that had held me prisoner for decades and been my residence during the darkest period of my life. But the thought of Rose venturing into their territory made my stomach churn.

"I think it's a good idea," I said. "But I don't want you coming."

She stopped soaping herself and stared at me.

"It pains me just thinking about it," I said. "Even with your ability to wield fire, after everything we've been through, I just want there to be a few days in a row when you're not facing mortal danger."

Silence fell between us. She cast her eyes away from me and finished washing herself. Then she stepped out of the shower, reaching for a towel and wrapping it around her. She walked up to me, placing her arms around my waist and resting her head against my chest. I held her closer, breathing in her scent.

"I think I would drive myself out of my mind staying here while you went without me," she said, "but, Caleb, if you don't want me to go, I won't."

I was shocked by her words. I'd expected her to reply with an argument, to be adamant that there was no way she wasn't coming. I hardly knew how to respond.

I reached for her head, looking deep into her green irises, and tried to understand what had brought about this sudden submissiveness. As the corners of her eyes moistened, I realized. Gone was even the slightest trace of the steely determination I'd grown accustomed to seeing in Rose Novak. She'd become putty in my hands.

Running my hands down her back, I pressed her against the wall. I dipped my head and closed my lips around hers. She breathed heavily, reaching her warm hands beneath my shirt and tracing her fingertips along my chest.

"I love you," I breathed, brushing my thumbs against the sides of her mouth as I continued to taste her again and again.

She responded in a hoarse whisper, "I love you," but she didn't need to. She'd just shown that her love for me was strong enough to overcome her nature as a Novak. She was willing to submit to my request to not cause me unhappiness, even though it pained her in equal measure.

Perhaps I'm now the only one who can tame the ball of fire that Rose Novak has become.

Even as I looked at her, my resolve ebbed away. Although I despised the idea of her riding toward danger once again, her submission was melting me.

A battle now raging within me, I scooped her up in my arms and carried her to the bedroom. I sat her on the edge of the bed, gazing down at her.

She looked up at me, her expression calm, her eyes wide with surrender.

I realized then that, even in our better days, Annora had never behaved like this with me. Although I loved Annora and would have done anything for her, I could hardly remember a single instance when she had put my desires before hers.

A storm of conflicting thoughts continued to whirl in my mind. On the one hand, I just wanted to do what was best for Rose. I wanted to keep her safe. But on the other hand, now I felt guilt stabbing me for causing *her* unhappiness by making her stay.

I swallowed hard.

You are impossible, Rose Novak.

After several more minutes of wrangling with myself, even though I hated myself for it, the softer side of me gave in. I bent down to her level.

"Okay," I said, taking her hands in mine. "Get dressed."

She frowned in confusion, her lips parting.

"Come with me," I said, even as I heaved a sigh.

"But I don't want to cause you pain," she said.

A smile crept across my lips. "As insane as it sounds, I'll probably be in more pain thinking of you and your sorry face left behind in this cabin while I'm riding toward danger by myself."

Her face lit up. Standing, she reached her arms

around my neck, drawing me in for another passionate kiss before she hurried to the closet to get dressed.

Chapter 23: Rose

Caleb and I rushed to Kiev and Mona's tree. I was glad to see that there was a small crowd already waiting for us there—consisting of my grandfather, Micah, Ibrahim, Gavin, and, to my surprise, Griffin. They stood alongside Mona and Kiev.

My grandfather looked at me with concern as I hurried up and gave him a hug. I was so sure that he wanted to request me to stay behind, but I was both relieved and surprised when he didn't. He just kissed the top of my head.

I turned to Griffin, raising my brow. He grinned at me. "I convinced my mom to allow me to come instead of her. I've been a vampire long enough now that I'm used to my strengths and abilities."

As for Micah, I wasn't surprised that he was here. His expression was one of determination. He'd been through hell at the hands of those witches. I was sure that he had been the first wolf to step forward and volunteer to help us.

"So," I said, looking around at each of them. "I suggest we head over to the dragons now."

We hurried through the forest toward the Black Heights. As we ran along the tunnels and reached the first corridor where all the dragons' apartments were, we found Jeriad along with several other dragons standing together and talking. They turned around to face us as we approached.

"Hello," I said tentatively. "Are you ready to accompany us?"

Jeriad eyed each of us, then nodded slowly. He shot a glance at the dragon standing beside him, who walked away and began knocking on doors along the corridor.

Soon, dozens of dragons were piling out of their quarters and walking toward us in the center of the corridor. Of course, the prince was not among them. I supposed that this was not a task for royalty. Once I counted about fifty, and it appeared that no more were coming, I pointed to the exit. We left the mountains and gathered in the clearing outside.

"You still haven't told us where exactly you want to go," Jeriad said.

"There are two islands not too far away from here," I said. "Islands governed by the black witches. They have stolen a number of humans—young men and women—whom we want to try and rescue. We are hoping that at least some of them are still being held there."

"Very well," Jeriad said after a pause. "None of us are fond of black witches. It sounds like this task will not be a difficult one to put our hearts into."

Without warning, the men started expanding. The eight of us backed up against the wall of the mountain to make space for the dragons as they assumed their full size. I craned my neck upward, looking for Jeriad. I spotted him about twenty feet away. Caleb and I walked straight to him. Jeriad reached out a massive hand and we climbed onto it. He lifted us upward so that we were level with his head. Caleb climbed up onto his back first, then held out a hand and pulled me up next to him. He sat behind the dragon's neck, and I sat behind Caleb, wrapping my arms around his waist and holding on tight. The others were beginning to mount dragons too.

"You should fly in front, Jeriad," Caleb said. "Out of all of us, I know best how to reach the island."

As Jeriad was preparing to take flight, Mona called up to me from below. "Rose, what are we doing?"

"What?"

"It will be much faster if I just magic us all there."

I felt like a fool for it to not have occurred to me. I was about to open my mouth to speak to Jeriad when the dragon shook his head.

"We fly there with you, or not at all," he said.

I cast a glance down at Mona, who was looking irritated. "It would be instantaneous if you would allow me to take you there."

Again the dragon shook his head. "No. We don't accept that sort of assistance from witches. We will fly."

Mona heaved a sigh, but didn't argue back. She climbed up onto the dragon Kiev had already mounted and sat behind him.

"We'll head to my island first," Caleb called to everyone. "Let's go."

The dragons' heavy wings beat the air and we launched into the sky with a jolt.

I already knew how fast dragons could fly. I estimated that it might only take an hour for us to reach there. Of course, it was more time than if Mona had just vanished us there. But for whatever reason, they weren't comfortable with that.

I didn't talk much to Caleb as we traveled. He needed to concentrate on making sure that we were all headed in the right direction. It had been a while since Caleb had visited that island. But he'd spent so many years in that dark place, I was sure that we would have no problem getting there.

It ended up taking one and a half hours before Caleb slowed all the dragons until they were just hovering in the air.

Caleb pointed directly ahead at what looked like nothing but more open sea. "Fly forward," Caleb said to Jeriad.

The dragon began moving forward. Then he stopped, as if his head had hit against something solid.

Caleb nodded. "We have reached the boundary."

We turned around to look at Mona. Anxiety was written on her face as she looked straight ahead. She let go of Kiev, and, levitating herself in the air, moved closer toward the boundary. She reached out her hands, laying them flat against it. She closed her eyes tight and her arms began to tremble. She uttered a chant. Five minutes passed in intense silence among the rest of us. All eyes were on Mona as she was lost in her own world, trying to crack the spell. Perhaps the strength of the boundary had increased since we had last visited. Perhaps it was so strong that even Mona couldn't penetrate it.

But my fears were unfounded. It took ten more minutes of severe concentration on Mona's part, but eventually her hands pushed through and she disappeared from sight. Although the island was still invisible to us, it appeared that she had broken down the protective barrier keeping people out.

She called from the other side of the boundary. "You can fly through now."

Jeriad and all the other dragons did as she had requested. A cold blast of wind hit my face the moment we entered. This island was still covered with snow and was as frozen as ever. But whereas previously I would've been shivering, thanks to my recent transformation, I didn't find the temperature disturbing. Sure, it was cold, but it wasn't painful.

There were several submarines lined up by the port. But so far, there was nobody in sight. The dragons flew beyond the port and began to touch down in the clearing just before the thick woods started. The area wasn't large enough for all of them, so when Jeriad landed, as soon as we climbed down from his back, he turned back into his human form. The others did the same until all of us were standing around the dark clearing.

Mona locked herself in a tight embrace with Kiev. She kissed him hard, then broke away and walked up to me.

"I'm sorry I can't stay. Your parents are depending on me—"

"It's not like you could do much even if we did find Rhys here," I said, "He overpowers you now."

She nodded, though she didn't look any less concerned. "I'm worried about how you're going to get to the other island without me."

"We'll manage," Caleb said with confidence I didn't feel. "We'll have to find someone here on this island we can bend into submission."

Mona sighed and cast one last glance at her husband before vanishing. The rest of us gathered closer together.

"Firstly," Caleb said, "we need to try to figure out whom we are up against." He addressed Micah. "You have the best hearing. Listen carefully, can you hear anyone up in the castle?"

Micah held his breath, his brows furrowing in concentration as he listened. He nodded slowly. "There are voices coming from there."

"Any idea of how many?"

Micah bit his lip. "Perhaps half a dozen people. It's hard to say from this distance. There are a number of voices overlapping each other. I can't hear Rhys among them though, or his sister and aunt. I'd recognize their voices."

"Okay," Caleb said. "Then we ought to assume the worst-case scenario, that all the black witches are here."

"Prisoners are usually kept right at the base of the castle, in the dungeons, correct?" Aiden said, addressing Caleb.

"Yes," Caleb replied.

"Then the dragons should cause a distraction in the upper levels," Kiev said, following their line of thought.

"You'd be able to do that, Jeriad?" I asked.

"Yes."

"You just need to be careful not to breathe too much fire until we've made it safely back out of the castle," I said. "Ibrahim will levitate up toward you to inform you once we've finished looking around inside."

Jeriad nodded.

"Okay," Caleb said. "Let's head to the stairs." He caught my hand and we all began running through the trees. Still falling behind Caleb's speed, I ended up just jumping onto his back and allowing him to carry me the rest of the way.

Once we arrived at the steps leading up to the towering castle, he addressed the dragons again. "Since you object to being transported by magic, I suggest you turn back into your dragon forms now and begin flying up toward the top of the castle. Ibrahim, in the meantime you should vanish us up the steps."

The dragons began transforming again while the rest of us huddled around Ibrahim, who vanished us all from the spot and made us appear just outside the door of the castle.

Shivers ran along my spine as I looked out at the view, my eyes traveling from the dense woods to the mountain peaks surrounding us, and then settling on the wide step beneath my feet. A rush of memories flooded my mind. I held Caleb's hand tighter. I remembered so clearly the night I had hugged Caleb, sitting right here on the step, looking down on the dark island. That same night I had lured him into dancing with me in his room, and I'd kissed him for the first time on his cheek. It seemed so long ago now, and yet it wasn't. I remembered how he'd tried to keep me locked up in my room. I hadn't realized at the time that he'd been trying to keep me safe.

Caleb squeezed my hand, glancing down at me as if he were experiencing the same nostalgia.

I forced my eyes back up to the sky. The horde of dragons was flying full speed toward the top of the castle.

"I don't hear anyone until at least halfway up the castle," Caleb said, his eyes narrowed. "Do you, Micah?"

Micah shook his head.

Caleb looked worried now. While this meant we would hopefully not bump into any of the residents, it was also chilling to realize that the humans likely weren't on this island. Surely if they were they would be making noise.

As if reading my thoughts, Caleb said, "We should check anyway."

I nodded, even as my heart sank into my stomach.

"They've started," Griffin said. He stood several feet away from us with his father, both of them staring up at the dragons.

Billows of flames were beginning to hit the turrets. Although they were far up, I could still feel the wave of heat rushing down, touching my skin.

"Keep your ears peeled, Micah," Caleb said. "Tell me what you hear."

"Footsteps, moving further up the castle."

"Then let's go." I urged. I looked nervously back up at the dragons. Hopefully they would heed my warning not to release too much fire just yet.

We all stepped back as Ibrahim stepped in front of the double doors and held out his palms. The doors blasted apart and we hurried inside. Goosebumps prickled my skin as I looked around the grand entrance hall—yet more memories resurfacing.

I could almost see the dark memories whirling behind Caleb's eyes as he took in the room.

He pointed to a door on our left. "Through there," he whispered.

Caleb led us through the door and slammed it behind us. He moved toward a trap door in the corner of the room and pulled it open. "There's no point in us all going down. Stay here while I look."

He disappeared into the darkness of the hole. My heart hammered in my chest as his footsteps faded. Caleb arrived back a few moments later.

"No luck," he said. "Let's head to the kitchen next."

We opened the door again and hurried across the hallway, darting into the kitchen. We snaked around the stainless-steel tables until we arrived at the entrance to a dungeon I was familiar with. Caleb had once carried me down here and locked me up with my parents. We entered and looked around, but it was obvious after a few seconds that it was empty.

"We're just fooling ourselves," Caleb said. "None of us can smell warm human blood in this castle."

"So what?" I said. "They're gone already? Where would they have taken them?"

"It's possible they've drained them of their blood already and stored it somewhere else. Otherwise, the only other place I can think of they could've taken them is their lair in the supernatural realm. The other side of the gate."

"Do we have time to search there?" Gavin asked.

"I don't know," Caleb replied.

"Let's just try," I said.

Since nobody objected, Caleb nodded. He led us out of the kitchen again and toward the entrance area. We darted into another chamber. Caleb bent down next to a carpet in the corner of the room and, pulling it aside, revealed another wooden door. He gripped the handle and attempted to pull it open. It was stuck fast. Caleb stepped aside, nodding toward Ibrahim. The warlock took the hint and stepped forward, casting a spell upon the door. That had no more effect than Caleb's pulling.

"Some kind of charm has been cast over this. It's

locked fast," Ibrahim said.

I bent down on the floor, placing my hands flat against the wood. "Why don't we just try to burn it?" I muttered.

"You can try," Ibrahim replied.

I was already beginning to summon the heat in my hands. "Stand back," I said.

Fire burst from my palms and enveloped the door. I stood up, watching the flames closely. They seemed to be disintegrating the wood. The black witches hadn't been very thoughtful in securing this door—I guessed they didn't expect to have intruders.

Once it looked weak enough, Ibrahim extinguished the fire, then slammed his foot downward against it. Sure enough, it fell away from its hinges and crashed to the floor. We lost no time in hurrying down the steps and into the dark chamber below.

"There's the gate," Caleb said, pointing to a circular hole in the middle of the floor.

Caleb leapt through it first, followed by me and the rest. We hurtled through so fast I could barely keep my eyes open. By the time my vision came into focus again, we had landed in another dark room. We stood up quickly, brushing ourselves off, and followed Caleb up another flight of stairs, toward a door that, thankfully, hadn't been charmed. Caleb was able to force it open himself. A dim orange streak of light fell upon us as we entered into some kind of large kitchen.

"Humans," Caleb said. "I smell them now."

The other vampires nodded in agreement, as did Micah.

"It's coming from..." My grandfather took a step forward as he sniffed the air. He walked further into the room and stopped outside another trap door. "Down there?"

"Yes," Kiev said suddenly. "I've been here before."

Caleb took a few steps back, still sniffing the air. "I sense human blood upstairs, too." He gripped my hand. "We need to split into two groups. Kiev and Micah, come with us upstairs. The rest of you, break into that dungeon. We'll meet you back down here."

Caleb ushered me onto his back. Since Ibrahim wasn't coming with us, we couldn't have me slowing Kiev and Caleb down even a little. They raced out of the kitchen with me and entered into a large hall next door. There was a flight of stairs in the center and we began racing up it.

"Why would they keep some humans separate?" I asked nervously.

"I don't know," Caleb said.

With each level that we climbed, I kept expecting that we would bump into someone. Finally, after what felt like the fifth level, Kiev and Caleb stopped climbing. They exchanged glances briefly and nodded.

We took a left and began jogging down a corridor lined with doors. I jumped at each creak of the floorboards as we hurried forward. Finally, we stopped short outside a door that was very different from all the others I had seen in this place so far. It was tinted red, and it had strange, intricate carvings etched into it—it looked like some ancient language.

Kiev's breath hitched. "No. We can't enter this room."

I gaped at him. "What do you mean?"

"This is a spell room."

Understanding sparked in Caleb's eyes. "Kiev's right. We can't go in here."

I wiggled off Caleb's back and placed my ear against the door. Caleb's hand closed tightly—almost painfully—around my arm. My voice caught in my throat as I heard whispering on the other side of the door.

"I can hear them," I gasped. "We just need to—"

"Even if we managed to open the door and get those teens out of there," Kiev said, "we wouldn't be able to save them."

"What?"

"They were doomed the moment they stepped inside." Kiev gripped my arm and pulled me back along with Caleb. "A curse is placed upon black witches' spell rooms. Any person who enters who isn't a black witch won't survive long."

My head reeled. "But those humans—" They were so close. They were just a few feet away. Their terrified voices rang through my head. It seemed to have grown louder, as they'd likely heard us talking outside.

Caleb and Kiev backed away from the door, pulling me with them. "There's nothing we can do for them, Rose," Caleb said. "We just need to try to save whomever we can downstairs."

Caleb guided me onto his back again. I clung to him, still in shock. Even as they began to hurry back down the corridor, I stared at the door. Those young men and women we were abandoning.

We had almost reached the staircase leading back down to the ground floor when a thud against the floor behind us made me jump. Caleb and Kiev stopped short, gazing around to see where the noise had come from.

Glowing in the darkness of the corridor behind us were three sets of red eyes.

Chapter 24: Rose

"Run!" I screamed.

But it was too late. Three giant wolf-like creatures emerged from the shadows, hurtling toward us so fast that Kiev and Caleb could barely react.

Caleb dodged them narrowly, leaping up with me on to the bannister a few feet away.

Vampire dogs. They were even larger than Shadow, their teeth sharp and long like knives.

Since when do black witches keep vampire dogs?

Kiev perched on a narrow windowsill opposite us. Two of the dogs leapt at Kiev again while another lashed out at us with razor-sharp claws. Caleb jumped with me onto the bannister on the other side of the staircase. The dog was moving so fast, Caleb could barely lash out at it. The dog was forcing us further down the staircase. Kiev hung from a chandelier, glaring down at the two dogs trying to bite at his legs.

"Put me down," I said suddenly.

Caleb ignored me as he continued trying to find an angle where he could make contact with the beast's eyes.

"Put me down," I said again. Heat was welling beneath my fingertips, the panic of the situation making it hard to control myself.

Caleb backed into a corner and allowed me to slide down onto the floor. Had the fire released from my fingertips even a moment later, my head would have likely been inside that beast's mouth. But a blaze of fire emanated from me, engulfing the dog completely.

I stepped around its burning form and rushed back up the stairs toward where we had left Kiev. To my horror, the chandelier was now a pile of smashed glass on the floor. One dog lay on the ground, whimpering and thrashing about. Its eyes had been slashed from their sockets. But the other dog and Kiev weren't anywhere in sight. Caleb caught up with me, gripping my arm.

"We have to find him!" I said.

Mona will never forgive me if something happens to him.

Caleb began leading me down the corridor. "I hear them."

When we reached the end of the hallway, Caleb pointed to our right. Kiev had wedged himself up the narrow walls like a spider, inches away from the dog snapping at his feet.

"Hey!" I hissed.

The dog spun round, its eyes fixing on me. It began charging toward me.

Once the dog was five feet away, I let loose another storm of fire. The creature's shrieks pierced through the silence of the castle. Kiev was limping as he made his way toward us. He had a nasty bite in his leg. *At least he hasn't lost another limb.*

"If there is any witch in this castle," Caleb breathed, wiping sweat from his brow, "they will sure as hell have heard us by now. We need to get out of here."

Caleb wrapped one arm around Kiev's waist since Kiev's wound hadn't finished healing itself yet, while I supported his other side.

We had almost reached the staircase when Caleb stopped suddenly. He looked at Kiev. "Can you hear that?"

I couldn't hear anything other than our own uneven breathing.

Kiev frowned, then nodded. "Someone is calling for help."

"Where?" I asked.

"It sounds much more distant than the spell room," Caleb said slowly. "Further up the castle."

"Could it be more humans?"

The two men shrugged. "Only one way to find out," Kiev grimly.

We all looked down at Kiev's leg. It was still bloody, but it was healing quickly.

I could tell that we were all thinking the same thing as we stared each other. We still didn't know if there were witches in this castle. But, considering the noise we had just made with those dogs, it wouldn't have taken long for them to manifest before us. The fact that no one had yet gave me hope that the castle was empty. We'd come this far, if there were indeed more humans higher up in this castle, we ought to at least try to help them.

"Come on, let's go quickly," I said.

We retraced our steps, back along the hallway, up the stairs, this time passing the level where the spell room was. We climbed higher and higher until eventually, even I started to hear the shouting.

On reaching the top of the last staircase, we stood on a small dim platform. There was a steel door in front of us. Caleb reached out and gripped the handle, pulling it downward. Squeaking, the door swung open. We stepped through it and found ourselves beneath a dark stormy sky. A harsh wind tinged with sea spray whipped against our faces. A black ocean extended all around us as far as I could see. We were on the roof of the castle.

"There," Kiev said. He pointed to a rectangular structure almost forty feet away. I could barely make out what it was in the gloom. But the cries became louder as we started approaching it. We reached the structure to find it covered with thick tarpaulin. Caleb and Kiev pulled it off to reveal five women, their faces pale and shining with sweat.

My mouth dropped open as I recognized one of them. With long white-blonde hair and clear blue eyes, she was unmistakable. *Hermia Adrius.* Sister of the Ageless. The witch who had only recently tried to kidnap me while I was standing on the mountaintop back in The Shade—moments before I had discovered my fire powers.

"You," Kiev hissed.

"Please, help us," Hermia said, her voice rasping.

Caleb gripped my arm. "Let's go, Rose."

Kiev had already spun on his heel and walked in the opposite direction, back toward the door.

"Wait," I said, even as I felt confused by my response.

I stared at the white witches' angst-ridden faces. I had more than enough reasons to despise them and want them to die a slow death, but there was something about the way they looked at me now that made it hard to feel hatred toward them. They just looked... pathetic.

"You have magic," I said, addressing Hermia directly. "Why don't you just magic yourself out of here?"

"We can't," Hermia said. "They cursed us with a spell that took away our powers before locking us in here."

"Rose!" Kiev hissed. He had reached the door and was holding it open. "Get over here, now!"

"I'm coming," I called. "Just give me a second."

I wriggled away from Caleb's grasp and approached the cage cautiously, careful to keep my distance.

"Why on earth would we help you?" I glared at Hermia.

She bit down hard on her lower lip.

"We helped you defend The Shade," the brunette

next to her piped up.

I scoffed. "Only because it benefited you." I looked again at Hermia. "Do you not recall trying to kidnap me just a short while ago?"

Hermia lowered her eyes to the ground, then nodded. "You have no reason to save us," she said, her voice cracking.

"Please," the brunette begged. "Please help us. You've no idea what horrors the black witches have in store for us."

"Rose!" Now it was Caleb getting on my case.

Why am I stalling? The side of me that was closer to my father was screaming at me to just go with the men and leave these witches to their fate. I had been known to listen to my father's instinct more often than not in the past, but, somehow, this time the other side of me—the side that was closer to my mother—came into prominence. I couldn't help but think that not even my worst enemy deserved the torture these white witches were about to go through at the hands of Rhys and his people. It just didn't feel *humane* to leave them here, caged like animals. Besides—ignoring the fact that Hermia had tried to kidnap me and the fact that the witches' actions were always only selfishly motivated—I couldn't deny that they had benefited our island by stalling the black witches' assault.

I took a deep breath, part of me still feeling crazy for even contemplating what I was about to say. "Even if I wanted to let you go, how would I do it?"

Hermia pointed to a small black cabinet fixed against the wall, near the door we had just exited from. "The keys are in there. They kept them purposefully close to taunt us."

"And if I set you free, where would you go? You're sure as heck not coming with us."

"I think there are some still some boats moored in the harbor down below," Hermia replied, hope sparking in her eyes. "We would try to escape back to our realm across the ocean."

I paused, contemplating her words. "And what reward would I get for saving an Adrius?"

Hermia looked at me anxiously. "My deepest thanks, and a promise that none of my kind will ever bother you again."

"I don't trust you to keep promises," I muttered.

Still, even though I was still mesmerized at what I was doing, I found my legs walking toward the wooden cabinet and opening the door. Reaching inside, I found an old rusty key and picked it up. Then I walked slowly back to the cage. I looked deep into Hermia's eyes.

"Don't make me regret this," I breathed. Sliding the key into the keyhole, I twisted it and the cage door popped open.

The witches stumbled out.

"Thank you," the five of them said at once, and I could've sworn that I actually saw sincerity in their eyes.

To my surprise, Hermia dropped to her knees before me and, reaching for my hands, kissed them both. She looked up at me, her eyes glistening with tears of relief. "I promise, Princess of The Shade, that I'll never forget what you have done for us. I will make sure that I, my sisters, and all those we rule over never trouble you or The Shade again."

She let go of me, casting one last lingering glance my way before all five of them hurried toward the edge of the roof. I wasn't sure what they were doing at first, but then I noticed the beginnings of a narrow winding staircase—apparently leading all the way down the side of the building. I watched the last of them disappear, then turned back to the two men who were staring at me, flabbergasted.

There was no time to explain the conflicted inner workings of my mind right now. "Okay," I said, heaving a sigh. "Let's get out of here."

We made our way back down the staircases through

the castle until we arrived at the ground floor. Crossing the room that led into the kitchen, we found the others already waiting there for us, a group of about twenty teens huddled in a corner. Their pale faces turned toward us as we entered the room. They scrambled even closer to each other.

"What happened?" my grandfather asked, running toward us and gripping my shoulders. His eyes fell on the blood staining Kiev's leg.

"We're okay," I said, "We need to just get out of here. But… these humans are the only ones you found?"

My father nodded sadly.

"Where are the others? I thought they stole over a hundred from that school. And those are just the ones we're aware of. We're missing so many."

Could they all be locked in that spell room?

"These people are all we've found, darling," Aiden said.

I looked at Caleb. His face was ashen.

"We need to try to get out of here now with those we've found," Caleb said. "If we stay here longer, we risk losing not only their lives, but our own."

"Maybe some others are kept in Stellan's island," I said hopefully.

"They took them upstairs," a weak voice spoke behind me. I turned to face the humans in the corner. A girl with wide brown eyes and curly black hair, no older than fourteen, had spoken. I walked over to her, bent down and touched her shoulder.

"U-upstairs?"

She nodded, flinching at my touch.

My stomach clenched. I swallowed back the lump in my throat and stood up, looking over the humans.

So we've lost the others. We just have to do our best to save these people now.

"I thought you looked upstairs?" Ibrahim said.

"They're being kept in a spell room," Kiev said.

Before more disturbing details could be discussed about the state of those humans in front of the ones before me, I addressed the group. "It's okay," I said, "We're going to get you out of here now. Please, stand up. We need to leave."

The poor teens were so shell shocked they struggled even to stand. We all gathered around them, helping them up, and herded them back toward the room that held the gate. Kiev entered last and bolted the door shut.

"Caleb and Rose," Aiden said. "Why don't you two go down first and wait for these humans at the other end? We'll make sure they get there safely."

Caleb and I leapt through. I held on tight to him as we hurtled down, wincing at the way my stomach somersaulted.

Landing on the other side, I knew immediately that something was wrong. Very wrong. The room was veiled with smoke, and the temperature was much higher than when we'd left. I climbed up and poked my head through the hole where the trap door had been. The door to the chamber above the basement was closed, but smoke was leaking through the bottom of it. I shot Caleb a panicked glance.

The dragons have been breathing too much fire.

The first of the humans began flying into the room, landing on the floor all around us. Several of them began coughing immediately at the smoke. About a minute later, everyone was through the gate. We all climbed up into the room above and I approached the door nervously. I opened it ever so slightly and peered through the crack. A wave of heat scorched my eyeballs, blurring my vision. I clasped a hand to my mouth. The entire entrance hall was ablaze. Walls of fire closed in around us, blocking the windows and the exit.

I slammed the door shut, choking, and looked toward Ibrahim.

"We're going to need water. Lots of water."

CHAPTER 25: ROSE

Two girls fainted behind us from the fumes. Griffin and Gavin picked them up and flung them over their shoulders.

"Hurry," I said.

Ibrahim rushed to the door and opened it slightly. More smoke spilled through. To my horror, he stepped right out and slammed the door behind him.

"What—?"

I hurried to the door instinctively and was about to open it to peer through, but Aiden held me back. "Ibrahim knows what he's doing. Don't open it again. We're suffocating enough as it is."

I pressed my ear against the door. "Ibrahim?"

I heard him muttering a chant on the other side, giving me relief that he was all right.

The door opened again about a minute later and this time, it wasn't to another wave of smoke. Cool air drifted inside. I looked over Ibrahim's shoulder to find myself looking down a narrow tunnel of flowing water, blocking off the flames on all sides and leading directly to the main exit.

Thank God we brought a warlock.

Ibrahim opened the door wide, then stepped back into the tunnel of water he had just created.

"It's safe to come now," he said calmly.

We ushered the humans out of the room and instructed them to follow Ibrahim in single file. He began leading them toward the end of the tunnel. Carrying two girls, Gavin and Griffin followed before the rest of us. The humans gazed around at the water in awe. I was sure that most of them believed that they were in a dream.

I heaved a sigh of relief as a freezing gust of fresh air blew through the entrance.

Soon we had all passed along the tunnel and were standing outside on the snowy steps. The teenagers were dressed mostly in T-shirts and shorts. They began to shiver.

We all looked upward. The dragons were still circling the turrets of the castle like a dark, deadly cloud.

"I'm going to go up there now and bring them back down," Ibrahim said.

Ibrahim vanished. When he reappeared again, he was high up in the sky, levitating beside the silver-orange scaled form of Jeriad. I watched them exchange some words and then they all descended to the ground. Several of the younger teens screamed as they noticed the beasts.

I hurried toward them, holding out my hands. "It's okay. They're not going to hurt you."

I doubted a single human heard my words amid their own screaming.

"Silence!" Kiev bellowed.

The teens fell silent instantly, their eyes now fixed on the grumpy green-eyed vampire in fear.

"It's okay," I repeated, even as the dragons touched down on the mountain. "They're here to help you, I promise."

Jeriad climbed over the rocks toward us.

"What happened?" Caleb called up to him.

"The witches didn't put up much of a fight," Jeriad replied. "They tried at first to protect the castle, but once they saw how many of us there were, they vanished... What took you so long?"

"Oh, long story," I said, casting a glance at the humans, who were shivering more and more with each moment that passed. The dragons' eyes shot toward them. Before any of the teens could start screaming again, I said, "We have to leave now."

"And go where?" Griffin asked, still carrying a girl over his shoulder.

"According to the news," Aiden said, "they were taken from California."

California. I looked from the humans, to the dragons, then back to the humans. I walked over to the teens.

"Uh... any of you fancy a ride on a dragon?"

Chapter 26: Rose

The teens were still too terrified to go near the dragons… understandably. They backed away as soon as I suggested going anywhere near the creatures.

"Jeriad," I said, straining my neck toward his towering form. "Would you mind changing back into a human in front of these humans? It will help ease their nerves."

Jeriad looked irritated at my request, but I was relieved when he granted it.

"Watch," I said, addressing the humans. "You will see in a moment that he's just a man."

They gaped as Jeriad's dragon form shrank, leaving

in its place a man—albeit an extremely intimidating man. After all the humans had the chance to stare at him, he assumed his dragon form again.

"There's no time for this," Caleb said impatiently. "We don't know that the witches are truly gone. We must leave."

He bent down and reached for the nearest human to him—a boy who looked about fifteen. He helped the boy onto his back, then gestured with a nod to Jeriad. The dragon lowered his hand for Caleb to climb up onto, then raised him onto his back. Caleb helped the boy wedge between the dragon's scales and leapt back down.

He glanced at the others. "Well? What are you waiting for?"

"At least two of us need to accompany the humans on each dragon," I said.

We set to work assisting the humans in climbing atop the dragons. Then the rest of us mounted.

"Hold on tight," I whispered to the humans now sandwiched between Caleb and me.

They looked dumbstruck as they stared down at the scales they were clinging to. Some of them yelped when the dragons launched into the air. Rising higher and higher in the sky, we glanced down at the burning castle—enveloped so completely I could barely make out a single patch of stone wall. The firelight flickered in Caleb's brown eyes as he stared at it. I couldn't imagine what it must've felt like for him to watch that place burn to the ground. I smiled at him when he finally turned to face me.

"How are you feeling?"

"Pretty damn good."

"Hey," Micah—now in his wolf form—barked from the dragon behind us. "What about Stellan's island?" He shared the same look of euphoria as Caleb in watching the castle burn. "I'd really like to see their base there burnt down too."

"We can't." Caleb gestured to the humans. "Firstly, we've got these people to drop off. Secondly, we don't have any way to get inside. We haven't captured any hostages."

I was sure that Micah expected that answer, but he looked disappointed all the same.

And so the dragons carried us away from the mountain range, over the woods, and toward the ocean. As we passed the boundary, it was dark outside now. The wind conjured up by the dragons' mighty wings combined with the cool sea breeze made me terrified that one of the humans was going to slip off into the dark waves. I looked over at Ibrahim, who was riding on the dragon parallel to us. "Is there anything you can do to make them more secure?"

He thought for a moment, then nodded. Less than a minute later, a thick rope closed around my waist. The rope expanded, wrapping around the girl in front of me, and continued until it reached Caleb's waist. Now we were all bound together on the dragon. I could breathe much more easily. I looked around to see that Ibrahim had done the same with everyone else.

Although it was still chilly, most of the humans had stopped shivering by now. An hour into the journey, several boys' and girls' heads began to loll. They must've been exhausted. I felt thankful that I had thought to ask Ibrahim to secure them.

Sitting at opposite ends on Jeriad's back, Caleb and I didn't say much for the rest of the journey. But I felt his gaze on me almost the whole time. The lightness of his mood that had come from witnessing the burning of his old castle hadn't left him even now. He was floating.

After a couple of hours, Caleb twisted round and faced forward. He began to give precise directions to Jeriad. After another hour, I caught sight of glimmering lights in the distance. We were fast approaching the shore.

"You see that beach there," Caleb said to Jeriad, pointing, "the one that's the most lit up? We should land there."

I patted the girl in front of me on the shoulder. Her head rested on the back of the boy in front of her. She was sound asleep. I shook her a little until she sat up straight.

"You're almost home," I whispered, squeezing her shoulders.

The beach was almost empty at this time of night. We crossed the last of the ocean and touched down on the sand. A couple who were walking by began screaming at the top of their lungs and racing away.

We couldn't remain here long. I doubted we had much time before dozens of people began swarming the beach to take a look at this bizarre spectacle. While I had a fair amount of trust in the dragons, after witnessing their behavior with our own humans, I didn't want to try their patience. I didn't know how they would react to these humans—they weren't residents of The Shade, after all.

Ibrahim vanished the ropes that had been fastening us all to the humans and we helped them down off the backs of the dragons as fast as we could. I was glad to see that the two girls Gavin and Griffin had been looking after had come to by now. They were looking around wide-eyed and anxious.

"Gather round," I called to the humans, beckoning them toward me.

"We need to contact the police," Aiden said.

"Why don't you, Ibrahim and Caleb come with me," I replied. "We'll take these people and the rest of you can wait here with the dragons."

Since there were no objections, we set off. Sand soon gave way to concrete, and we found ourselves standing at the side of a busy road. I looked straight ahead on the opposite side. There was a line of restaurants.

We crossed the road carefully while herding all the teens and reached the other side. Aiden led us into the nearest restaurant to us. It was packed with diners. There was no way that all the humans would fit in here, so I suggested that I go in while the men waited with the teens outside. I pushed open the double doors and headed straight for the welcome desk.

"I need to contact the police urgently. May I use the phone?"

The woman behind the desk parted her lips in surprise, then nodded and handed me a phone. "Of course."

I dialed the emergency code. As soon as I was

connected, I explained that I had with me over twenty missing people. I gave the name of the restaurant, then hung up.

"Thank you," I said to the woman.

She was still gaping at me as I hurried out of the restaurant.

"Well?" Caleb asked as I emerged outside.

"They're coming." I turned to the teens. "It won't be long now until you're back with your parents. The police are coming."

The teens already looked much more relaxed being in this familiar environment, and now they were positively beaming.

I was impressed that we had to wait barely five minutes. Cars pulled up all around us and uniformed police officers hurried toward us. They headed straight for the teens, except for one—a tall caramel-skinned woman with short cropped hair. Her eyes traveled from me to each of the men, then back to me.

"You are the person who called?" she asked.

I nodded.

"Your name?" she asked.

I was about to blurt out my real name, but I wondered whether that was wise. Of course, it wasn't like these police knew about the Novaks, but all the same, I decided I preferred anonymity.

"Alice Jenkins," I said, offering a hand to her. She shook it firmly.

"Ms. Jenkins, we're going to take you and these gentlemen in for questioning. Please step this way." She pointed back to her vehicle.

I shot Ibrahim a glance, and he nodded. None of us wanted to get entangled in a lengthy interview process, so we all huddled closer to the warlock. I cast one last lingering glance over the teens just before we all vanished.

We reappeared again on the beach. I was shocked to see how quickly the situation had escalated. Swarms of humans were now surrounding the dragons, although they were keeping a fair distance. They all had their phones out as they took pictures and recorded footage.

Micah and the three vampires looked relieved to see us as we approached. The dragons, still in their giant forms, were looking irritated by the flashing. Before more people could arrive, we climbed back onto the dragons and they took off again into the sky. Gasps of awe erupted from the beach below. Climbing closer to Caleb on the dragon's back, I wrapped my arms around his waist and looked back at the glimmering shoreline. Although my heart was warmed to imagine those teens returning to their parents, I couldn't help but feel grief for those we had left behind. And for those the witches had yet still to make victims out of. For those we couldn't save.

The work we had done tonight was just a drop in the ocean.

"We have to end Lilith," I whispered.

CHAPTER 27: DEREK

After letting the hunter go, I left the alleyway and walked back toward the beach. I found Corrine with Sofia beneath the shade of a cluster of trees, where I had told them to wait.

"What happened?" Sofia asked, looking me over anxiously as I approached.

I gathered her to me, holding the back of her head and placing a kiss on her forehead. "I dealt with him."

"So it really was a hunter?" she asked.

I nodded. Caleb had told us about the fracas he'd had with the hunters on his way to try to rescue us from Annora's curse. It really was no surprise that an organization had formed again after Aiden had shut it down about two decades ago. There had been too many victims since then thanks to the black witches' vampires.

"Did you kill the bastard?" Corrine asked.

"No. I just gave him a good shaking. He won't shoot so carelessly next time he sees a vampire." I placed an arm around Sofia's waist and looked at the witch. "Let's return now, before there are any more distractions."

Corrine grabbed hold of the two of us and barely three seconds later, we were gone. Once the air stopped rushing around us, the familiar sight of the Port came into view. "Let's hope that by now Mona has come up with something." I imagined that the black witches might be stealing more teenagers as I spoke.

"Why don't we visit Xavier and Vivienne first?" Sofia said. "It's on the way."

But when we arrived at my sister and brother-in-law's apartment, nobody was at home. Since Aiden's tree was the next one along, we checked in there. He wasn't at home either. We were about to head for Mona and Kiev's after that when someone shouted down at us. We looked up to see Zinnia waving from Eli's balcony.

"Come up here!" she yelled.

We hurried up the tree and Zinnia grabbed Sofia's arm as soon as we exited the elevator.

"Zinnia, what—?"

She dragged us through Eli's front door. The living room was packed with people. Their backs turned toward us, they all seemed to be focused on the television.

"Guys," Zinnia said, "they're back."

Two dozen people spun around to greet us. I noted Xavier and Vivienne right at the front near Eli. Then my eyes traveled further along the room and fixed on the screen. Sofia, Corrine and I gasped at once.

I squinted, pushing my way through the crowd closer to the television, believing that my eyes must've been mistaken. But they weren't. Sofia and I knelt right in front of the screen, so close that the glare hurt my eyes.

We were looking at a sandy beach crowded with dragons. Several men in dark clothes stood next to them, and surrounding the group were swarms of humans.

The woman reporting the scene on the television seemed lost for words as she stammered and stuttered her way through trying to describe the situation.

As the camera zoomed in further, I could clearly make out the features of the men standing right by the dragons. Kiev, Griffin and Gavin. Now I also spotted a wolf sitting nearby—Micah, it seemed. Corrine clasped a hand to her mouth, kneeling down beside us.

Before any of us could voice our bewilderment, Zinnia spoke. "As you can see, some of us left the island—my boys included. Rose got it into her head that we ought to storm the witches' islands in search of the humans."

"Rose? Did she go, too?"

"Yes."

I glared at Xavier and Vivienne, who looked like they were steeling themselves. "I didn't give anyone permission to leave before we returned," I said. "Especially not Rose. Why would you have let her go?"

Vivienne stood up and walked over to me, placing a hand on my shoulder. "Calm down. Rose is safe. They all arrived in California—Ibrahim, Caleb and Aiden went too. The reporter just mentioned before you entered that about two dozen teens have been dropped off at a nearby police department."

I sat back down in front of the screen, my eyes fixed once again on the dragons. It was all so surreal. We had just returned from visiting several police officials, informing them of the existence of supernaturals. Seeing these huge dragons lined up on the beach like this, surrounded by swarms of humans snapping pictures, pointing, and talking animatedly amongst themselves… it was the most graphic representation of what I'd feared the moment I laid eyes on Ben's footage on the news: a timeless barrier had been broken.

Things would never be the same for the human world again.

CHAPTER 28: MONA

It killed me to leave Kiev, Rose and all the others on that island without my assistance. But I had to. I didn't know how long it would take them, and Derek and Sofia—hell, this human realm—was now depending on me to find a way to get rid of Lilith. Enough time had been wasted already with the dragons' stubborn insistence on flying instead of allowing me to magic them all there.

As I vanished myself back to The Shade, I just reminded myself that even I was not much use against the black witches anymore. I remembered how effortlessly Rhys had overpowered me. They had the dragons. I couldn't offer any better protection than those beasts.

On arriving back in The Shade, I didn't speak to anyone. I headed straight for Kiev's and my treehouse. I walked into the kitchen and poured myself a glass of cool water. Swallowing it down in a few gulps, I wiped the sweat from my brow with a kitchen towel. My palms were cold and sweaty as I gripped the tabletop hard, my knuckles whitening.

How am I ever going to do this?

I had already told Derek that I knew little about Lilith. Yes, I had met her, but Rhys had deliberately withheld details about her. I left the kitchen and began pacing up and down the living room.

Think.

I spent years and years living with those black witches. During that time, I must have witnessed some conversation, picked up on some clue that could help me now.

Lilith. That abomination of a living being. How is it that she survived all this time when no other Ancients could? I had a feeling deep in my gut that if I managed to answer this question, I would discover the key to Lilith's undoing.

Time is running out. I don't have all day to just stand here and pace.

There was only one thing to be done right now. I

vanished myself from the spot and reappeared in the Sanctuary. Since I hadn't yet set up a spell room in Kiev's and my apartment, I had no choice but to use Corrine's.

I began rummaging through Corrine's shelves and pulling down bottles of ingredients. I reached for a medium-sized cauldron that was drying by the sink and began tipping substances into it. After adding enough liquid, I sped up the heating process until the potion had reached a rolling boil. I relinquished the heat and poured the liquid into a jug. Tidying up my mess in the space of three seconds, I left the kitchen, clutching the jug in my hands. I reappeared again in my apartment. I headed this time straight for the bedroom and placed the potion on my bedside table. I manifested a goblet from our kitchen and poured out one full portion. Then I climbed on top of the mattress and slid between the sheets, propping my head up so that I was sitting at a forty-five degree angle. I reached for the goblet and took a sip. The liquid burned my throat as it slid down.

As the memory potion began to take hold of my mind, I fixed all my consciousness on one single question: *Why is Lilith still alive?*

My vision now beginning to cloud, I closed my eyes. I felt a tingling sensation in my head, like the feel of blood trickling beneath my skin. And then my present mind was no more as I was transported to the past.

Chapter 29: Mona

It was the beginning of a bright summer's day, the best kind of weather The Sanctuary had to offer.

I sat up in bed, yawning and rubbing my eyes. I swung my feet off the mattress and padded over to the mirror in the corner of the room. I reached for my brush and began combing my long hair—as I had promised my mother that I would do first thing each morning if she allowed me to grow it this long. Then I walked into my bathroom and took a shower. I had to hurry. I was expecting my best friend, Rhys, to knock at my door early. He always did on the weekends, when we had no classes to attend.

Sure enough, I had barely slipped into my clothes and

tied my hair up in a ponytail when there was a banging on the front door. I shot out of my room and whisked down the stairs before my parents or my siblings could answer the door. I always liked to be the first to answer the door to Rhys, because my parents made it no secret that they didn't like me hanging around with him.

Rhys was standing on my doorstep, wearing a black shirt and shorts. He was barefoot. A mischievous grin lit up his face. "You ready?"

"Yeah," I said, slipping out of the door and closing it as softly as I could behind me. We raced down the front steps, across the yard and out into the street behind the front gate.

"You should have been there last night," Rhys said as we jogged along.

"Yeah, well, I think I'll prefer it during the daytime."

After picking up two of our friends along the way, we finally reached the graveyard. The main gates were still locked, so—still being young and not yet having mastered the ability to disappear and reappear in a different location—we climbed over them and leapt down to the ground behind it. Then we all set off running again, racing to see who could reach the back of the graveyard first. Rhys won, as he usually did. He was the fastest runner among us.

"Hey!" an angry voice called as we reached the back of the graveyard. "You don't have permission to go there!"

I groaned internally. Shamus, the caretaker. The elderly warlock draped in a black cloak manifested himself in front of us. He blocked our way, waving a finger.

"We're just looking around," I said.

Before Shamus could react, Rhys darted between his legs and dove into a cluster of bushes. I wasn't sure what to do. I didn't want to get in trouble, but I also didn't want to be left out of Rhys' game.

I tried to follow after Rhys, but the warlock held me and my other two friends back, pinning us to the ground with his magic.

Rhys' taunt filled the early-morning air from the other side of the bushes. "Come and get me."

My eyelids fluttered as I came to consciousness for a few seconds. The first memory subsided. I sank under again…

The graveyard was pouring with rain, the skies overhead gray and cloudy. Crowds of witches and warlocks piled in through the gates. A new tomb was being installed here today—that of my friend's grandmother, Hetia. Children were allowed to the front of the ceremony so they could watch what was happening, so my parents allowed me to push through the crowds without them. I joined my friends at the front and we all watched as a long black coffin was lowered into the ground. By the time respects had been paid, the rain was falling so heavily that the grave had become a pool of muddy water. Hetia's family had to dry it out before they covered it over with a tombstone. Then they bent over the grave and began etching letters into the stone—ancient characters that I couldn't understand at my young age.

I barely surfaced even for a second this time before another seemingly random memory took hold of me.

I was on my knees, a scrubbing brush in my hand, a bucket of soapy water set beside me on the ground. I looked around at the sea of tombstones surrounding me. I hated this job. I swore to myself that I wouldn't misbehave in class again or do anything to deserve this punishment. It irked me that my other classmates had been misbehaving too. I had been unlucky to get caught.

I heaved a sigh, brushing my hair, sticky with sweat, away from my forehead as I continued scrubbing the Ancients' tombstones. Some of them were so covered with grime, I was sure that nobody ever cleaned these things. Perhaps they kept them so dirty purposefully, so as to keep them as a worthy punishment for troublemaking children.

At least it was daytime. Although the sun beating down on me was making me feel nauseous, I was glad at least that I didn't have to come here at night. This part of the graveyard, right at the back, always felt more haunted than other parts when the sun went down…

Now a fourth memory began playing in my mind's

eye.

I was drowning in a pool of rancid liquid. The more I tried to swim to the surface, the thicker the liquid seemed. Just as I reached the surface and gasped for air, something sharp and bony closed around my ankle and dragged me downward. I was pulled further and further into the depths of the black pool. My lungs close to bursting, I felt like I was seconds from death. But then I was met with an unexpected reprieve. My head was raised out of the liquid and I was able to breathe. Choking and spluttering, I tried to get rid of the vile taste in my mouth. Still in darkness, I reached my hands all around me, feeling stone.

I tried to push against the low ceiling, but it wouldn't budge. Then there was a crack. A gap formed above me. I pushed against the ceiling once again, discovering that this was no ceiling. It was a lid. It slid right off, allowing me view of a clear night sky overhead. I heaved myself out of the liquid and found myself rolling onto grass. Looking around me, still shaking, I realized that I had just climbed out of a grave. I was surrounded by tombstones. I stood up and realized that I was in The Sanctuary's graveyard.

I looked back at the grave I had just climbed out of. My voice caught in my throat as Lilith's rotten face glared up at me, her beady black eyes gleaming through the darkness.

I sat bolt upright in bed, panting.

How could I have been so stupid? How could this

not have been the first thing that occurred to me?

The graveyard.

When I had killed the Ageless, Lilith had taken me through some kind of portal connecting her rancid pool to a tombstone in The Sanctuary. A tombstone I now believed had been *her* tombstone. I couldn't believe I'd had to take a memory potion to make me realize this. I supposed that this was an episode of my life that I had just driven deep into my subconscious and tried to forget.

Fighting off another bout of memories, I hurried to the kitchen and drank a large cup of water. This would help to dilute the potion in my system faster and return my mind to its normal state. I'd remembered enough, at least for now.

I entered the hallway outside the kitchen and stared at the front door.

I'm going to have to go back to The Sanctuary. And I'm going to have to go alone.

I grabbed a piece of paper and a pen and scribbled a quick note for Kiev. I knew how unhappy I would make him by leaving without him. But I simply couldn't wait. After placing the note down on the dining table, I hurried back to our bedroom and pulled out the map I had procured of all the gates leading into this realm. After studying it for several moments, I had worked out the best route.

Looking around the bedroom one last time, I vanished myself.

Chapter 30: Mona

Arriving on the beach outside the borders of The Sanctuary's royal city, I shuddered. After my last visit here, I hadn't ever expected to return. I scanned the beach. Nobody was in sight, but I made myself invisible all the same. I couldn't afford to be spotted. Not now.

I walked across the sand toward the trees that lined the beach, where the boundary started. Once I could walk no further, I stopped and stretched out my palms. Being a Channeler, I hoped that I still had enough strength to bypass the boundary—something no ordinary witch could do. I was relieved when after about five minutes, I managed to. I could tell that they had put some extra reinforcement around the island since I'd last been here, but it still wasn't enough to keep me out.

It was nighttime now and the forest was almost pitch black as I made my way toward the city. I could have magicked myself there, but I wanted to walk. I needed some time to clear my head and arrange my thoughts before thrusting myself right into the heart of the witches' realm again. The trauma of my last visit here still haunted me.

I wondered what the white witches' plans were now, after they had failed to protect The Shade. I wondered whether they would try to do anything further to stop the black witches. Whatever the case, we certainly couldn't rely on it.

Although I was nervous making my way toward the city, I also couldn't help but feel a sense of lightness. I rolled the ring on my finger. Whatever was about to happen, I didn't believe that the pain could be any worse than when I was last here, when I had believed that I had lost Kiev.

Once I reached the first main street, I decided to travel the rest of the way by magic. I knew the graveyard's gates would be locked at this time of night, so I reappeared behind them. It was uncanny being here now, when only hours ago I had experienced this place in my memories. As I looked around, it hadn't changed at all—even since I was a little girl.

I took in the sprawling mass of tombs. The moonlight cast a pale glow down on them. I began making my way toward the back of the enclosure, past the newly departed toward the most ancient tombstones. These graves were larger and longer— much longer—than all the others in this place. I couldn't count the number of graves that were here for the Ancients. There were far more than in the front area.

I slowed down as I caught sight of Lilith's tomb about ten feet away. Chills ran down my spine, the hairs on my arms standing on end. As I neared it, I kept half expecting it to spring open. My nerves were grateful that no such thing happened. The tombstone looked quite dead, just like the rest of them. I placed my palms over the lid, running them over the moss-covered stone.

So I'm here.... Now what? What am I waiting for?

I knew why I was stalling. I wasn't ready to find Lilith herself yet. If I did discover her now, I wouldn't stand a chance against her. What I needed to do first was figure out how to destroy her.

Still, my subconscious had directed me to this grave.

Perhaps I would find some clue by opening it up…

It didn't help that it was the dead of night. An owl was hooting in a nearby tree and some kind of insect I couldn't put a name to hummed eerily.

Taking a deep breath, I did my best to brush aside my fears. I got my fingers beneath the ridge of the lid and began to pull upward. It was stuck tight.

I took a few steps back, then began uttering a chant. I was shocked at how easy it was. After my first attempt at a spell, there was a crack and the slab loosened. My throat parched, I inched closer, bracing myself for what I was about to see. I bent down and pushed off the lid. It fell to the grass with a dull thud. I found myself staring down at a bed of soil.

I looked around the edge of the slab to check that I had gotten the right one. I had. This was Lilith's.

I was still fearful, but I had come this far in opening up the grave, I wasn't about to close it again without getting to the bottom of it. Using my magic, I dug deeper and deeper. Part of me was still expecting to reach liquid at some point, but there was nothing but soil and when I did finally hit something, it was the lid of a mahogany coffin.

I stared down at it. Then, holding my breath, I went the final step and popped open the coffin's lid. It was empty. The sheet that had likely once enveloped Lilith's body was crumpled up in one corner.

I'd come to this place in hope of finding answers, but now my mind was flooded with more questions. I could only conclude that the connection Lilith had made with this place had not been permanent and was created at her will.

Lilith had once been buried. Had she actually been dead? Or had she faked her death? I could hardly believe that it could have been the former. I didn't think that it was possible to bring someone back from the dead.

Frustrated, I covered up the coffin with earth and replaced the slab.

What now? Go back to The Shade and try to invoke some more memories? Memories that might just lead me on another wild-goose chase...

I was beginning to feel more hopeless than ever. I found myself wandering around the tombs nearby, kicking dirt as I racked my brains for my next move.

As I walked along, my eyes fell upon the etchings on the graves. They were only just visible beneath the grime that coated all the Ancients' tombs. The writing was old witch tongue.

The names of the witches within the tombs were scrawled in large font, and beneath them were lists of between three to five departed friends or family members. It was witch tradition to spell out which late loved ones one wanted to rest with after death. I walked back to Lilith's tomb, curious to see whose names she had wanted etched upon her grave. Although I had visited this tomb before, at the time I had been in too panicked a state to pay attention to what was written on her grave. Heck, I hadn't even made the connection that this was her grave to begin with.

I scraped away the moss, and was surprised to see only one name. And not even a full name. It just said:

"Magnus."

As it was the custom to write both birth and death dates of the departed witch who lay within the tomb, it was also the custom to inscribe the birth and death dates of those loved ones whom they wanted to rest with.

I began scraping away beneath the name *Magnus*, now curious to see when he had lived.

But just as his name was incomplete, so were his dates. There was a birth date… but no death date.

Odd. Very odd.

Who was Magnus? I could only assume that the lack of death date meant that Magnus had still been alive when Lilith was buried. Although his birth date was far before even Lilith's birth. He would have been a very, very old warlock.

I furrowed my brows, trying to recall if I had ever learnt in history classes about anyone significant called Magnus. I couldn't.

I realized that I was procrastinating. I shouldn't have been taking so much interest in something that was probably irrelevant, but right now I was parched for ideas, so I let my mind continue on this tangent.

I found it bizarre that Lilith would have requested someone to be written on her stone who was not even dead yet. I'd never heard of a witch requesting a living person to be written on their slab. That was considered bad luck.

My mind felt like one big jumbled-up puzzle. Too many pieces with no rhyme or reason as to how to put them together.

I have wasted enough time here already. I should just return to The Shade and try to invoke more memories that will hopefully be of more value than those graveyard ones.

Still, as I kept staring down at that single name with no death date, I couldn't help but feel that this might be the closest I might come to a clue, no matter how many liters of memory potion I drank.

CHAPTER 31: MONA

I felt crazy even for thinking it, let alone acting on it. But I did. I decided to stay overnight in that terrifying graveyard. I just couldn't bring myself to leave The Sanctuary—the only place where I had any chance of discovering some clue about this Magnus person—until I had at least tried to find out about him.

It was custom for the caretaker to come early each morning and clean away the moss from the newer graves up front by the gates. I wouldn't have been surprised if it was still old Shamus on duty.

So there I found myself, huddled against a tree as close to the front gates as possible. Of course, I couldn't sleep. I couldn't shut my eyes even for a moment without feeling jittery. I just kept my gaze on the gates, waiting patiently for the caretaker to walk through once the sun peeked above the horizon.

As it turned out, I was waiting longer than dawn. At least sitting here wasn't so unbearable once the sun was shining. I was actually starting to enjoy the view. The graveyard was situated on a hill and it overlooked the sparkling ocean.

Judging by the position of the sun, it was almost noon by the time the gates swung open and an old warlock appeared. Indeed, it was Shamus. He looked no less grumpy now than he had all those years ago. Once he had closed the gates behind him, he made his way toward the first grave. I stood before him and relinquished my invisibility spell. His face paled as if he had just seen a ghost.

"Y-You?" His face scrunched up as he squinted at me.

Clearly, he recognized me as the outcast and traitor that I had been labeled again by the white witches. Before he could vanish and inform anyone of my presence, I arrested him with a spell, pinning him to the spot.

I held up my hands. "I am not going to harm you,

Shamus," I said. "I just need to ask you a few questions. Then I promise that I will leave this place."

He glared daggers at me, but since he had no other option, he nodded.

"I'm going to give you control of your mouth again, but you must promise that you won't scream or shout. If you do, I'm going to be forced to shut you up again… and perhaps take more drastic measures. Do you understand?"

He nodded again, his blotchy face reddening with fury.

It was too risky to stand with him here right by the gates. I moved us toward the back of the graveyard, reappearing right in front of Lilith's grave. I pointed down at the etchings on the stone.

"Do you know anything about Lilith?" I asked. He certainly looked haggard enough to have been around long enough to know at least something about her.

"I know a little," he growled.

I pointed to Magnus's name. "Do you know who this person is?"

"Lilith's loved one, obviously."

"Why is there no death date here?" I asked.

"Most likely Lilith only provided us with the birth date and did not know when he died."

"Could this person have still been alive when Lilith was buried?"

Shamus scoffed. "Do you honestly think that an Ancient would have gone against such a basic custom? Of course he must've been dead."

"Then how could we have not known the death date? The Council records births and deaths of every single resident of The Sanctuary. The information is etched onto all the other graves here—"

"Perhaps Magnus did not live in The Sanctuary," Shamus said. "Perhaps he lived outside."

"Outside…" I muttered. "Then Magnus wasn't a warlock?"

Shamus rolled his eyes. "You always did strike me as a dimwitted one. Of course he must've been a warlock. Just because he lived outside The Sanctuary doesn't mean he wasn't one of us. In the Ancients' time, there were a number of reasons why witches and warlocks would be stationed outside." He shook his head in disbelief that I should even ask such a question. "It's considered treasonous even now for a witch to have a relationship with anyone but their own kind, not to speak of in those times…"

I paused, wondering if Shamus' words were really true.

"I have answered your questions," he said. "You should leave."

I looked at the warlock, then nodded.

"Okay, I will."

As promised, I released him and vanished myself away from the graveyard. But I was not yet ready to leave The Sanctuary. I reappeared on the beach outside the boundary again, making myself invisible as I sat down on a cluster of rocks. I stared out at the calm ocean as speculation after speculation flooded my brain as to who and what Magnus really was.

CHAPTER 32: MONA

I realized that there was one sure way to find out Magnus' identity—or at least to confirm whether he was a warlock, as Shamus had insisted upon. If he was one of us, then he must have been born in The Sanctuary. This was another rule strict followers of the Ancients abided by. Even if a witch was stationed outside, she was required to give birth to her child within the confines of The Sanctuary.

I waited until night had fallen before standing up and dusting myself off. I penetrated the boundary once again and this time I headed straight for the Council's meeting hall, within the Adriuses' castle. As expected, the room was empty at this time of night. I walked across the hall and stopped above a trap door in one of the corners. Climbing down through it, I was glad to see that this basement still served as the witches' archives. There were shelves upon shelves of leather binders and countless cupboards and cabinets filled with documents. It was all neatly labeled and organized, so it didn't take me long to find what I was looking for—the birth records section. I already knew the date of Magnus' birth, since that had been written on the tombstone, so I soon located the right shelf. I flipped through the month he'd been born in. There wasn't a record of any Magnuses born then. I flipped through the parchment a second time, just to be sure I hadn't missed anything, before replacing everything neatly.

So, Lilith had loved a man called Magnus. But he had not been a warlock.

This alone was intriguing. I was shocked that Lilith could've broken such a fundamental rule.

I didn't know what exactly the relationship between Lilith and Magnus had been, but she'd held enough affection for him to want to list him as the only person on her tombstone.

Now that I thought about it further, she hadn't provided a surname for Magnus either. Perhaps there was a reason for that. Perhaps Lilith had wanted to give as little information about him as possible to avoid him being identified. She'd hoped that people would just assume he was a warlock, as Shamus had.

I returned to my spot on the beach and sat down again, rubbing my fingers against my temples as I tried to process this new information.

I grappled with the idea that a person with as black a heart as Lilith could be capable of loving anyone at all, much less a non-warlock. I never would have guessed that she would be able to experience such emotions.

I recalled the ritual Lilith had performed to turn me into a Channeler. Rhys had made it clear that the only way for it to work was for me to be accompanied by someone I loved. I had been too nervous at the time for this to strike me, but now that I thought about it, I realized just how bizarre it was. Love and emotions never came into the equation with black witches. It was all about duty and service to a higher cause. The fact that Lilith relied on the power of love to perform such an important procedure as creating Channelers seemed to be at odds with everything she and the black witches stood for.

What I wouldn't give to get inside that twisted woman's head...

My breathing became heavier as soon as I had the thought. Unwanted memories resurfaced, memories of that day in Lilith's cave when she had turned me into a Channeler. When she had probed my mind, seeing my every thought, my every fear, my most cherished memories... my palms grew sweaty as I remembered how violated I had felt to have her dark presence touching the deepest part of my consciousness.

I shook away the memory, attempting to bury it again, as I always did whenever I recalled that day. But then something made me stop. A sudden flash of recollection—a vision that had entered my mind during those hours I'd been trapped in the cave. A vision that had not been a memory of my own.

A pale brunette young woman with dark brown— almost black—eyes, sitting in front of a mirror and staring at herself.

Although I'd tried to forget everything about the day I'd visited that cave with Rhys, it dawned on me that I had to stop trying to forget. I had to start trying to remember.

Could it be that, as she'd had full access to my mind, I'd had access to hers?

At the time I had been so overwhelmed by her presence in my mind and then afterward I had been so desperate to forget... what I had witnessed from her side had never truly sunk into my consciousness.

I shot to my feet.

I need another memory potion.

Chapter 33: Mona

I didn't want to go all the way back to The Shade to use Corrine's spell room, and since it was still dark, it was safe for me to enter the city now and try to find a solution. I tried to think which potion room would be stocked with the greatest variety of ingredients. None would compare to the kitchen of the Adriuses. I already knew where it was located, so once I'd passed through the boundary, I vanished myself straight into the large chamber.

It was the most beautifully designed and well-stocked potion room I had ever been in. A witch's paradise, this room made Corrine's pale in comparison. I found all the ingredients I needed to whip up the memory potion in no time.

Once the potion was ready, I poured it into a jug and returned to the beach.

I had made this memory potion much stronger than the one I had taken earlier. I would need to probe into those memories I had fought so hard to lock away. Although witches didn't often walk along this beach, and especially not among these rocks, I couldn't take any chances. I would be unaware of my surroundings while under the influence of the potion. I looked around and spotted a little cranny in the side of the cliff about fifty feet away. I hurried toward it, careful not to spill any of the potion in the process, and was pleased to see that it was just the right size for me to slip into. I climbed inside and huddled as far back as I could. Stretching out my legs, my back leaning against the wall, I placed the jug between my legs.

This time before taking a sip, I focused all my concentration on the question: *What memories of Lilith did I access that day in her cave?*

Reaching for the jug, I took the first sip. I almost choked from how strong I had made the formula. Leaning my head back against the rocks, I closed my eyes.

The vision of her cave came flooding back, the dim lanterns casting shadows around the walls, the rancid smell of her pool, the claustrophobic feel in the chamber from lack of oxygen. I saw myself kneeling before Lilith, her bony hands closing in around my skull…

A young woman sat before a mirror in a large circular bedroom. She wore a long black dress that covered her feet and extended to her wrists. Withdrawing a silk cloth from one of the drawers in her dressing table, she wrapped it around her head and tied it in a knot. When she stood up, her frame was tall and slender. Her forehead creased as she stared at her reflection.

A voice called from outside the room. "Lilith."

The brunette stood up and opened the door. Another brunette entered the room.

"Sister," she said, clutching Lilith's shoulder, "What is taking you so long? We are waiting for you."

"I'm sorry," Lilith replied, her voice slightly hoarse.

Lilith's sister caught her hand and pulled her out of the bedroom, into a corridor outside. They vanished and reappeared outside, on top of a grassy hill. It was nighttime, and there were no clouds in the sky. The moon shone down, thousands of stars glistening. A tall older-looking woman was standing several feet away, gripping the back of a chair that had been set atop the soil. Sitting in this chair was a girl, blindfolded and gagged.

*The older woman beckoned the two girls over. "Shana,"
the woman called, addressing Lilith's sister. "Stand next to
me." Shana did as requested. "Lilith, pick it up." She
pointed to the ground and as soon as she did, an ax
manifested. Lilith's hands seemed to tremble slightly as she
stared at the sharp blade.*

*"Yes, Mother," she replied. Taking a step forward,
Lilith gripped the handle and picked it up.*

"Good," her mother said. "You know what to do now."

*Lilith nodded, her lips parting as she fixed her eyes on
the blindfolded girl.*

*Shana and her mother began uttering a chant while
Lilith continued to inch forward until she was barely a foot
away from the girl, who appeared to be unconscious. Her
head lolled to one side, but she was still clearly breathing.*

*Raising the ax, Lilith swiped the blade across the girl's
neck, severing her head with one swipe.*

*Lilith dropped the ax to the ground as blood began to
spout from the corpse's neck. She dipped her fingers into the
fountain of blood and painted two crosses either side of her
cheek. Then Lilith traced an octagonal shape on her
forehead.*

*The two women finished chanting. Lilith's mother
stepped forward, resting hands on Lilith's shoulders. She
smiled. "Happy birthday, my daughter. May you have*

many more years to come..."

My eyes fluttered open as the vision disappeared. I stared straight ahead, trying to make sense of what I had just witnessed. Then I took another sip from the jug and allowed myself to sink back into Lilith's memories.

Lilith, now dressed in a flowing emerald-green gown, stood in the corner of the palace's ballroom with her mother and an older man who appeared to be her father. Lilith was clasping her gloved hands nervously together, shooting fleeting glances at the dancing couples around the room. Several crystal chandeliers hung from the ceiling, casting down a warm glow upon the revelers beneath.

"They have arrived," Lilith's father said, pointing to two men who had just walked through the entrance. Lilith and her parents stared at the men—apparently father and son. They had light blond hair and grayish eyes, and the same broad shoulders. The younger blond man's eyes fixed on Lilith as soon as he caught sight of her. They weaved their way through the crowd and arrived in front of Lilith and her parents.

The father held out a hand to Lilith's father. "Meet my son, Crispian," he said.

Lilith's parents shook hands with Crispian, but Lilith seemed to be avoiding the young man's gaze. Her eyes were fixed on her feet. Her mother nudged her and only then did she raise her eyes to look briefly at Crispian. She held out her hand, allowing Crispian to take it and kiss the back of it.

"Would you care to dance?" Crispian asked.

Lilith glanced up at her mother, then nodded. The young blond man smiled, while Lilith's eyes remained cold, as Crispian placed an arm around her waist and guided her toward the dance floor.

Surfacing once again, I didn't bother to open my eyes this time. I just pressed the jug to my lips and swallowed another deep gulp.

The sun shone overhead, the warmth of the afternoon bringing a slight blush to Lilith's pale cheeks. She stood in the center of a rose garden wearing a white wedding dress. She pulled the veil down over her face, fixing her gaze straight ahead at the flower-covered gazebo just beyond the garden. Crowds of witches were settling themselves into the rows of seats in front of a raised platform at the back of the shelter.

White rose petals had been scattered on the ground to form a path leading from where Lilith stood up to the platform where a handsome blond warlock stood dressed in a smart gray outfit.

Lilith began to make her way slowly toward the groom. Her knuckles were white as she clutched a bouquet of flowers. Her lips formed a smile that did not reach her eyes. On reaching the platform, she looked down at the sea of faces. As they exchanged vows, Lilith's voice was shaky. Crispian looked down at her adoringly, slipping a ring on to her finger and pushing his lips against hers.

Then the scene faded away, being replaced moments later by a bedroom. Lilith—still in her wedding dress— and Crispian stood together in the center, surrounded by a circle of red candles. Crispian had his arms around his bride while she rested her head against his chest. They swayed gently from side to side. Then Crispian manifested a knife in his hands. Holding Lilith closer against him, he ran its tip down the back of her dress, splitting it open. He rolled her sleeves down her shoulders, discarding the dress, before deftly cutting away her undergarments. He took a step away from her, his eyes roaming her bare form for perhaps the first time.

"Sit," he whispered.

Folding her long legs beneath her, she obeyed.

Crispian knelt on the floor next to her and picked up one of the candles. He swirled it around gently, loosening some of the warm wax. Sliding his hand into her hair, he tilted her head backward and dripped a thin line of the red wax from her chest down to her navel. Then, picking her up in his arms, he carried her over to the circular bed and laid her down before proceeding to undress himself. As he began to make love to her, Lilith's eyes remained distant.

I took another sip of potion…

Lilith wore a black cloak, her hood pulled up as she ran along one of The Sanctuary's cobblestone roads. Her breathing was heavy and uneven as she ran. She didn't slow down until she'd exited the city, passed through the suburbs, and arrived at the beach. She collapsed to her knees, digging her hands into the sand.

"No," she whispered to herself, her face contorted with anguish. "I can't leave again."

She looked around, as if scared that someone might've heard her. She staggered to her feet and approached the ocean. She bent down and splashed water over her face. She bit down on her lower lip, shaking her head furiously as though she was having an argument with herself. She seemed to lose her own battle, because barely moments later, she heaved a deep sigh and vanished. When she manifested again, she appeared to be in the middle of a dense forest, so dense that barely a single ray of the moon could trickle down through the towering canopy above. Nevertheless, she launched into a sprint, racing harder and harder until the trees began thinning.

Soon she reached the end of the forest and found herself standing in a grassy clearing at the edge of a cliff. Her face shining with sweat, her eyes wide, she looked around. She whirled around at the sound of a snapping twig.

"So you came." A deep voice spoke from the darkness of the trees behind her. A tall man with pale skin stepped into

the clearing. Like Lilith, he wore a long cloak, his hood pulled up over his face. I could barely make out his features in the shadows but for two bright blue eyes. Lilith remained rooted to the spot as he stepped further into the light of the moon, closing the distance between them. Slowly, he lowered his hood, revealing cropped black hair.

"I shouldn't have come," Lilith breathed.

"Then why did you?"

Tears glistened in the witch's eyes.

Passion ignited in the man's gaze. His arms shot out and he pulled Lilith against him, dipping his head and claiming her lips. Lilith flinched at first, but then she eased into his embrace. She wrapped her arms tight around his neck, pulling herself closer. His large hands traveled down her back, one resting on her right hip while the other bunched up the hem of her dress and slid beneath it, brushing against her thigh. Breathless, she gripped his hand and stopped it from traveling any further.

"No," she whispered. "No. I came here to tell you that I can't see you anymore."

The man stared at her. "Why?"

"What do you mean 'why'?" Lilith snapped, even as her voice broke. "You know what would happen if I was caught with a vampire. I have disgraced my kind enough as it is."

He gripped her hands. "You love me."

She winced.

He let go of her, growling in frustration as he turned to look down at the sea of treetops beneath the cliff.

She called after him, her voice faint and weak, "I'm sorry... Magnus."

Magnus. A vampire.

To my frustration, the vision vanished. *I need to find out more about this man.* I was about to drink more potion when, to my surprise, another vision began overtaking me. I leaned back and closed my eyes.

Two elderly women, together in a room. One lay on a bed, apparently sleeping, while the other sat alongside her holding her hand. Incense burned on the windowsill, causing a light haze in the room.

The resting woman's eyes shot open. She tried to sit bolt upright, but the other pushed her back down.

"Lilith," she gasped, twisting her head to face the woman next to her.

"It's okay, Shana. It's okay." The now aged Lilith patted her sister's hand.

"I am sure that I won't make it through the night," Shana said, her eyelids fluttering. "Don't leave my side."

"I won't," Lilith said.

"Promise you'll stay here with me like I stayed for Mother and Father," Shana said.

Lilith nodded stiffly. Shana wheezed and coughed up a

mouthful of blood, which Lilith cleaned up with a flick of her hand.

"I just had... the most frightful vision." Shana gripped her sister's hand so tight her nails made dents in Lilith's skin. "I saw our future generations going astray. Growing complacent and neglecting all that we have worked for. Rejecting the very purpose of our existence... They will bring ruin to us all."

Lilith placed a hand over Shana's forehead. "Just rest now," Lilith said.

Shana shook her head. "No. I can't." She looked Lilith straight in the eye. "You must hold on for as long as you can. It's too late now for me and the rest of our generation, but you... you must try to hold on. I-I believe you were meant for this, sister."

Lilith grimaced, guilt showing in her haggard face. Her jowls wobbled as she shook her head. "You of all people know that isn't true," she replied. "I am a disgrace to our kind."

Shana scowled. "If you are truly sorry for the mistake you made, then now is the time to redeem yourself... Live on. One of us must."

"But even if I wanted to, how would I?" Lilith asked.

"Find a way... If you don't, then nobody will." Shana gripped hold of Lilith's arms and pulled her closer toward her until Lilith's nose was but an inch away from hers.

"Find a way, and this will be your redemption... Take the mistake you made and turn it into an advantage. You know the binding power of love... especially in Magnus' case. He is an immortal."

The warm glow of the bedroom disappeared along with Shana, and now the elderly Lilith was alone, crouched down over a cauldron in the center of a small grimy chamber. She stirred furiously as the liquid bubbled, fire licking the sides of the vessel and making her break out in a sweat. She began to recite a spell. Her words echoed around the room, her voice growing louder and louder, until the entire room was filled with thick smoke that was billowing up from the liquid. It became so dense that Lilith disappeared from sight.

But that haunting chant still echoed in my ears as I emerged from the memory. I played it over and over in my head, afraid that I might forget it. Scrambling to my feet, I crawled out of the cave and inscribed the chant on a slab outside. I stared at the words—now able to absorb them by sight as well as by hearing. Each time my eyes traveled across the words and each time they rang through my head, their meaning sank deeper, my understanding becoming clearer, until finally it dawned on me.

There were still questions that remained unanswered, but there was one secret I had now uncovered:

Lilith had used her love for an immortal to keep herself bound to this world for so long. That was how she clung on when others faded away.

Magnus is the reason Lilith is still here.

Chapter 34: Caleb

When we arrived back in The Shade, the dragons dropped us off near the Port before returning to their mountain homes. Aiden suggested that we head straight for Rose's parents' home to see if they had returned and, if so, inform them of everything that had just happened.

We didn't make it that far, however. As we passed Eli's penthouse, a number of voices drifted down from it—Derek and Sofia among them. Ascending in the elevator and arriving at the front door—which had been left open—we walked inside and found the living room packed with people. All of them were centered around the television set, which was displaying a scene of our visit to the beach. As soon as I'd seen those humans flashing their cameras, I'd suspected it wouldn't be long before mainstream media picked it up.

"You're back," Sofia exclaimed, rushing toward us with Derek. She wrapped her arms around Rose before allowing Derek a turn. Then the two of them looked at the rest of us.

"Well? Tell us what happened," Derek said.

Derek and Sofia sat down on the sofa with Rose in between them and she began to recount everything we had just been through. Every now and then, she would glance at me for support, and I would fill in details where she wanted me to. About halfway through, Ibraham stood up.

"I need to go see Corrine."

Corrine. All throughout our journey back from California, as I had traveled with Rose's warm body pressed against mine, I had been thinking about how I needed to pay a visit to the witch. With Rose occupied here with her parents, I realized that this would be the perfect time. I stood up and motioned to follow the warlock. Rose looked up at me questioningly.

"I will see you in a bit, Rose. I'm stepping outside for some fresh air."

She nodded, before continuing to recount our story.

I caught up with Ibrahim on the balcony before he could vanish.

"I would like to have a word with your wife," I said.

"Uh, okay. Come with me then." He placed an arm on my shoulder and vanished us both to the Sanctuary. My breathing quickened as I followed Ibrahim in through the door, and I realized that my hands were shaking slightly.

"Corrine!" Ibraham called along the corridor.

"Ibrahim?" Corrine's voice emanated from a room nearby. She raced out from a door and ran along the corridor, hurling herself at Ibrahim. Their lips locked in a passionate embrace. I looked down at the floor, taking a few steps back as they finished greeting each other.

"You must tell me everything," she said.

"And you must tell me," Ibrahim replied. "But Caleb here wants to speak to you about something first."

I raised my eyes to the witch. "I'm sorry to disturb you."

"That's quite all right," Corrine said, curiosity in her eyes.

Ibrahim continued along the corridor while Corrine gestured to a room to my right. A living room. I took a seat in an armchair while Corrine sat opposite me. But as soon as my backside touched the cushion, I realized that it was foolish thinking that I could remain seated for this conversation. I stood up and walked over to the mantelpiece, running a finger along the wood. I turned around slowly and fixed my eyes on Corrine.

My chest felt tight.

Just spit it out.

"I wanted to ask you… how might a man procure a ring on this island?"

Corrine's face lit up as soon as the words left my mouth. She leapt to her feet and hugged me.

"An engagement ring?" she asked, squeezing my shoulders.

I nodded.

"Do Derek and Sofia know yet?"

"I spoke with her father."

"Oh, goodness. My Rose, getting married… That girl is going to be over the moon." She sat back down in her chair and, reaching toward the coffee table in the center of the room, picked up a notepad and a pencil. "Do you have any ideas about how you'd like the ring to look? Any colors, shapes or stones in mind?"

In truth, I hadn't thought about such details. I sat down opposite Corrine. "I am not a jewelry designer. But I want something… bold for Rose."

Corrine smirked. "Let me see what I can do."

She sketched away on her pad for the next five minutes. I waited patiently, watching her design take shape. She lifted up her notepad, showing me the final result.

"Yes," I said instantly. "That's the ring for my girl. How long will it take you to make?"

"Well, when are you planning to propose?"

I paused, unsure of how to answer. The witch saw through my silence. "Let me just work on this now so you have it. It won't take me too long. My discussion with Ibrahim can wait..."

"Thank you."

She left the room, leaving me alone. I stood up again and began pacing.

Although there was no doubt in my mind that Rose loved me, and the fact that her parents had not objected was a weight off my shoulders, somehow I couldn't keep my stomach from clenching at the thought of proposing to her. A nagging voice at the back of my head kept telling me that it was too soon. That I ought to wait longer. That she was still so young. Girls of this day and age typically waited much longer before tying the knot than girls of my time.

Yet amid all these doubts was a determination I

could not shake: I wanted to make her fully mine, and I didn't want to wait any longer to do it.

I was so lost in my own thoughts that I almost didn't notice Corrine enter the room half an hour later. She was carrying a gray silk pouch in her hands. As she approached me, she placed it in my palm. I opened up the pouch and pulled out the ring—far more stunning than her sketch of it. Made of what appeared to be pure silver, it was encrusted with a gorgeous red ruby. I could already picture how beautiful Rose's hand would look with this adorning it.

"Thank you," I said again.

There were tears in the witch's eyes as she smiled. "It's my absolute pleasure... There is one thing that I simply must ask before you leave though." Her eyes roamed my body from head to toe. "Were you planning to look like *that* when you ask her?"

CHAPTER 35: ROSE

After I finished telling my parents and everyone else in the room what had happened to us while we were away, it was my parents' turn. They recounted their trip to North and South America, ending with their encounter with a hunter.

Silence filled the room as we finished talking.

"Mona… Has there been any update from her?" I asked.

My father looked toward Kiev, who was sitting a few feet away from him. My father reached into his pocket and pulled out a crumpled piece of paper. Unfolding it, he handed it to Kiev.

"As you will see from the note, Mona left the island."

I stood up and hurried over to Kiev, looking over his shoulder at the note.

"She didn't say where she's gone?" Kiev stared at my parents disbelievingly.

My mother shook her head.

Kiev stood up, anguish in his eyes.

"It seems that she didn't speak to anyone before she left," my mother said. "Derek and I went looking for her after arriving back on the island. We visited your penthouse. The door was unlocked but she wasn't at home. We just happened to find that note lying on the dining table."

"Dammit," Kiev breathed. He balled his fists, crumpling the note, and stormed out of the room. My heart ached for him. He had been through so much recently. The last thing he deserved was to be separated from Mona again. Yet I couldn't help but feel hopeful at the witch's note. It seemed like she was onto something. Otherwise why would she have left the island?

"Let's hope she returns soon," I muttered. There were so many people in this room, I was starting to feel claustrophobic. I decided to follow Caleb's lead and step out for some fresh air.

"I'll catch you later," I said, waving toward my parents as I headed for the door.

I wasn't even halfway across the room before my father whizzed past me and planted his feet on the floor in front of me.

"Where are you going exactly?"

"Just… outside. I'll join Caleb."

My father obviously didn't have the heart to chastise me for leaving the island given that we'd managed to save some humans, but he looked disturbed all the same. His electric-blue gaze pierced through me. "I don't like the way you keep slipping through my fingers, Rose."

I didn't know what to say. I just looked at him. He stepped aside, though I could feel his eyes still on me as I left Eli's apartment.

I made my way down to the forest ground but, before going to find Caleb, I decided to go and talk to some of my human girlfriends. I hadn't gotten any time alone with them since the ball, and I was dying to know what they'd thought of those dragons. I headed straight to the Vale and, on arriving in the town square, I caught sight of three girls sitting by the fountain, chatting with each other. As I neared, I recognized them as Sylvia, Becky, and Jessica.

"Hey, Rose!"

They each gave me a hug.

"How are you?" Sylvia asked.

"I'm okay. A bit exhausted… I haven't seen you since the ball. How did it go with those guys?"

Sylvia and Jessica giggled as they exchanged glances.

"That's just what I was asking them about," Becky said. "All I can say is that if I wasn't so in love with Griffin, I would definitely be in the market for a dragon." She winked at me.

"You saw what went on at the ball," Sylvia said. "As for what went on in our confidential meetings"— Jessica's and Sylvia's faces flushed bright red—"well, they're called confidential for a reason."

"Oh, okay. Fair enough," I said. "I guess what I really wanted to ask was whether or not you like them."

"Are you kidding?" Jessica said. "Tyron has ruined me for life. No other man will ever compare." She sighed dreamily. "He *redefines* the word gentleman."

"Good," I said. "I will be interested to know how your second meeting goes with them too. You have dates tomorrow, right?"

Jessica nodded enthusiastically. "We were supposed to meet today. But Jeriad informed us that they had to postpone it for tomorrow."

"Okay," I said. "Well, see you around."

Although I'd suspected that the girls would be bowled over by the dragons, I still felt relieved to hear it from their mouths. As I made my way back out of the Vale, I couldn't help but wonder exactly what had happened during those private talks… and if indeed talking was what had gone on.

I turned my thoughts back to Caleb. I called out his name once I reached Eli's tree again, but he didn't respond. I guessed that meant he wasn't in the area. *We'll bump into each other sooner or later.*

Instead of going to seek him out, I continued walking alone in the forest. I replayed the events of the past twelve hours over in my head. Before I knew it, I had arrived at the Port. I walked to the edge of the jetty and sat down, dangling my feet above the calm waves. I still couldn't shake the feeling of how uncanny this all was.

The human world knows about supernaturals.

I tried to imagine what the consequences of this might be. And I wondered whether the day would ever come when The Shade was discovered. I shuddered at the thought.

I almost jumped as a deep voice spoke my name. I twisted around to see Caleb standing behind me.

Something about him looked... different. It looked like he'd had a shower, for sure, but his clothes also seemed different than what I was used to seeing him wearing. He wore a white long-sleeved shirt, rolled up to his elbows. The first three buttons of the shirt were undone, giving me a peek at his muscled chest. He wore dark pants with a brown leather belt around his waist. Something about his appearance reminded me of a windswept sailor. Yet he was well groomed at the same time. His dark hair touched the sides of his face and he still had a shadow of stubble around his jawline, giving him a rugged, sexy look—but it looked a little tidier than usual.

Windswept sailor... Perhaps this is how he used to dress when he was aboard his family's ships.

Whatever he had done, he looked handsome as heck. I found myself breathless beneath his warm brown gaze.

A smile formed on his lips as, wordlessly, he walked up to me and held out a hand. I took it and he pulled me to my feet. I looked at him questioningly. He just continued to hold my gaze as he slid his hands down my waist and rested them on the small of my back. He leaned in, breathing in my scent deeply as he pressed his lips against the most sensitive part of my neck, just beneath my ear. His kiss was slow, tender, intense, his mouth remaining against my skin even as he began leading me into a dance. I felt my cheeks flush red as he finally raised his head, the expression on his face now serious as he stared deep into my eyes. My heart beat against my chest like a drum. I gulped.

"Uh… Hello, Caleb."

Still, he didn't respond. He just remained with his gaze fixed on my face, as though he were committing my every detail into his memory. Since there was no music, I tried to imagine in my head what tune we might be dancing to. Whatever tune it was, when it finished, Caleb slowed us to a stop. His hands slid down my arms and stopped at my hands, allowing me to twine my fingers with his.

I cocked my head to one side. *What is all this, Caleb?*

Finally, he broke the silence.

"You are my life now, Rose," he said. "Barely a minute goes by when I'm not pinching myself that I'm here with you. But I want to be here with you. I want to be here with you all your life, however long that might be…"

The blood pounded in my ears as Caleb let go of my hands and lowered himself to one knee. He pulled out the most beautiful ring I had ever seen in my life. Coated with silver and studded with a fiery ruby, it dazzled even in the pale moonlight. My breath hitched. My eyelids grew hot as tears began to well behind them.

"Caleb," I gasped.

"Rose," he said, his voice husky, his brown eyes never leaving mine. He took my hand and placed a gentle kiss over the back of it. "Will you marry me?"

My heart drowning in joy, I barely knew what I was doing as I grabbed his hands and pulled him to his feet. I hurled myself against him, wrapping my arms around him as tightly as I could and crushing my lips against his, as if trying to meld my body with his.

Clearly, he hadn't been expecting such a forceful reaction on my part. The sudden weight of my body against him sent him staggering back and we both fell with a splash into the ocean. I feared for a moment that he might've dropped the ring, but he hadn't.

"Should I take that as a yes?" he asked, his voice tinged with laughter.

"Yes," I choked, even as I swallowed a mouthful of seawater.

A grin splitting his face, he held out the ruby ring and slid it onto my finger. His hands found my hips and, sliding my body against his, he raised my head higher above the waves. I caught his lips in mine and kissed him again and again, the seawater on my face mixing with my tears.

Caleb hauled us both out of the glistening sea. He laid me down gently on the wooden floorboards of the jetty. His hands either side of my shoulders, he crouched down over me and tasted my mouth, his tongue brushing against mine.

Playfulness sparked in his eyes as he drew away and flicked back his soaking wet hair. "Well, Aunty Corrine's efforts didn't last long…"

Chapter 36: Aiden

Ever since Claudia had told me that Adelle had broken things off with Eli, I couldn't stop feeling guilty about it. After all, I was the cause of his pain.

After returning to The Shade, I spent some time with Kailyn, and then I decided I couldn't put it off any longer. I needed to visit Adelle and, for the first time since I'd known her, have a completely open and straightforward conversation with her.

But I didn't want to do this without first talking to Kailyn about it. I didn't want to hide any of this from her any longer.

We were both sitting on the front porch enjoying the

view of the island. My arm was wrapped around her while she rested her head on my shoulder.

"Kailyn," I said softly. "I need to talk to you about something."

"What is it?" She raised her head and looked at me.

"Everything I'm about to tell you, you must promise to keep to yourself. You mustn't tell anyone, especially not Eli."

"You can trust me."

I breathed in deeply. "It's about Adelle. She recently broke up with Eli… I suspect because of me."

Kailyn's eyes widened.

I placed my hand over hers. "I believe she has affection for me, perhaps has had for some time. When she saw me with you that day on the cliff, I believe it brought her feelings to the surface in a way that she's finding hard to handle."

I could tell from her expression what question she had in her mind now: Did I love Adelle?

I saved her the pain of asking. "I… I can't deny that not so long ago, I was besotted with Adelle. Due to unlucky timing, I never asked her out. I had been intending to, but I was too slow. Eli got to her first." I leaned forward and kissed Kailyn's warm cheek. "But then you came along. I choose you over Adelle, Kailyn.

And the only reason I'm telling you all this about Adelle is because I didn't want to hide it from you. I didn't want you to find out later on somehow and think that I wasn't being fully honest with you."

Kailyn nodded, giving me a small smile. "I appreciate that, Aiden… but how do you know that she dumped Eli because of you?"

"Adelle visited me some days ago, here in this cabin. She expressed that she held deeper affection for me than him."

"Oh."

"Do you mind if I go and visit her? I feel I need to close things off with her. Adelle needs to understand that I have moved on and not hold out hope. I'm hoping to persuade her to forget me and get back with Eli."

"Of course, Aiden. You don't need my permission to go and see her."

"Thank you." I drew her closer and kissed her lips before standing up and walking down the steps.

I wound around the mountain cabins in our area until I had reached Adelle's doorstep. Despite myself, I felt butterflies in my stomach at the thought of her standing there.

Get a grip, man.

I climbed the stairs and rapped against the door. Then I took a step back and held my breath. Footsteps sounded behind the door. There was a click and it swung open. Adelle stood before me, wearing a nightdress, her long auburn hair braided and hanging down one shoulder. I could tell that she had been crying; her eyes appeared glassy, her eyelids red.

She looked shocked to see me.

"Aiden?"

"I'm sorry if this isn't a good time. But we need to talk."

"O-okay." She stepped back and allowed me entrance. "Take a seat."

I sat down on the sofa while she sank into an armchair opposite me.

My heartbeat quickened even as I looked into her blue eyes. "Adelle, I'm going to tell you now what I've never told you before... what I held back during all those years we spent together as friends. I loved you. Deeply."

Her cheeks flushed red, her eyelids fluttering. She looked down at her feet.

"Had you not started going out with Eli," I continued. "I likely would've asked you out. You may remember, soon after you started dating Eli, I was avoiding you. You wondered how I even knew that the two of you had gotten together because you said you hadn't told anyone yet. I'd said that Yuri had told me. That was a lie. I walked in on the two of you embracing in the lakehouse."

Her lips parted.

"And do you know why I was there that day? Because I had intended to finally express my feelings to you."

I breathed out. A wave of relief rushed through me. It felt almost therapeutic to be finally letting this all out. I'd bottled it up for so long.

A silence fell between us.

"I-I didn't know that you loved me, Aiden," she said quietly. "You never gave me reason to believe it. From your behavior, I thought you were deliberately keeping me at a distance. Keeping me as your friend. I remember one time—perhaps that was the first time you had intended to ask me out—you had come to meet me outside the school, and you had wanted to take a walk with me down by the lake. Do you remember that?"

I nodded. Of course I did. That was the first attempt I'd made. But Ben had called from "Scotland" and thrown me off.

"I really thought you might have said something

then," she continued. "But the fact that you didn't convinced me even further that I was imagining things. Since you had given me no reason to believe that you saw me as anything other than a friend, I was afraid to voice what I felt for you, because I didn't want to ruin what we had. But now, it just seems that you were afraid… as I was."

I ran a hand down my face. *So she did have deeper feelings for me even then.*

"It's unfortunate, Adelle." I said. "But I didn't come here to just discuss the past. I came here because I need you to understand that… I'm with Kailyn. I have moved on. You should too."

She bit her lower lip, nodding slowly.

"Eli is heartbroken," I said. "You two seemed great together. Why don't you return to him?"

Adelle blew out a breath. "I told him that I needed some time apart. I didn't tell him that I had stopped loving him. I do still love him. It just didn't seem fair to him to stay with him even while I was having these feelings for you. It felt like I was deceiving him, even cheating on him somehow. It was dishonest. Before I can move back in with him, I need to sort myself out."

I nodded. "That makes sense, I suppose. But I do hope that you will return to him."

She reached into her pocket and pulled out a tissue, wiping a tear that had spilled down her cheek. Then she gave me a watery smile.

"Well, I'm glad you came by. It was good to talk. I-I can't pretend that I don't still hold feelings for you, but somehow it feels like a weight off my chest that we are no longer hiding things."

"I agree." I stood up. "And I hope after all this, we'll be able to resume our friendship even if it never becomes anything more than that."

She nodded, standing up too. I headed for the door and opened it. I stepped down onto the porch, looking up at her once more. We held each other's gaze for a few moments. Then she stepped down, touched my forearm and planted a chaste kiss on my cheek.

My heart hammered against my chest, whatever blood I possessed rushing to my cheeks.

Adelle's cheeks also grew rosy. "I hope you didn't mind. I've just wanted to do that for the longest time."

My voice caught in my throat. I backed away down the stairs. "Goodbye, Adelle."

"Goodbye, Aiden."

Chapter 37: Derek

Now that the rest of our council members and my daughter had returned from yet another wild escapade, I called another meeting in the Great Dome.

Sofia, Corrine and I recounted in detail our visit to the police to those who hadn't yet heard about it. This led the discussion toward speculating on the repercussions of humans and supernaturals clashing on such a wide scale for the first time. I had already mulled over the situation so much in my mind, I found myself tuning out and losing myself in my own thoughts.

When the door burst open and Mona stormed inside, I sat bolt upright.

Kiev shot to his feet and enveloped her in an embrace. She drew away from him quickly. Her hair was disheveled, her face sweaty, as her eyes traveled around the room, falling upon each of us.

"Do any of you know a vampire called Magnus?" she asked, panting.

"Magnus? What? What happened?" several of us asked at once.

She gripped the edge of the table and sat down. "Just answer my question."

There was a silence as each of us stared at her disbelievingly, then began racking our brains.

"Magnus who?" Vivienne asked.

"I don't have a surname," the witch replied. "But I do know that he must be a vampire old enough to have been alive during Lilith's youth."

"I knew a Magnus," Kiev said suddenly. "He visited the Blood Keep briefly during my stay there, a long, long time ago."

Mona gripped Kiev's forearm, shaking it. "And?"

Kiev's eyes narrowed as he called on his memory. "He was also a child of the Elders, like me. He would certainly have been old enough to have been around in Lilith's younger years…"

"But if Mona doesn't have a surname, how do we

know this is the same person?" Sofia asked, her brows furrowed.

"Describe the Magnus you knew, Kiev," Mona urged.

"He was, uh, tall. Short, darkish hair—at least at that time. I can't remember his eye color clearly now... blue, perhaps."

Mona nodded. "I do believe that's him."

"But what is all this about?" I asked, no longer able to contain my impatience.

She stood up and began pacing up and down. "I accessed Lilith's memories."

Kiev's jaw dropped. "Huh?"

"When she made me a Channeler, a bond formed between us. As she probed my memories, I also had access to hers. I took a powerful memory potion to force me to recall them." Mona stopped pacing and looked directly at Sofia and me. "We must find Magnus."

"Find him? Why? What if he's no longer alive?" We all began asking questions at once again.

Determination blazed in Mona's eyes as she answered, "Magnus must still be alive if Lilith is alive."

"Baby," Kiev said. "Slow down. You need to explain what the hell you're talking about."

"Lilith was in love with a vampire named Magnus," she said. "She used that love of an immortal to bind her to this world."

"Lilith's immortal?" Sofia gasped.

"No," Mona replied. "She's not immortal. Binding herself to an immortal's love has allowed her to extend her lifespan far, far past its natural length, but it will wear off."

"When?" Zinnia asked.

Mona scoffed. "I have no idea. But we can't afford to wait around for it to happen naturally."

Kiev looked at Mona in disbelief. "That creature, you're telling us that she's capable of… love?"

I was surprised to see a flicker of melancholy cross Mona's face. "Indeed, she is," she said, her voice softening. "The love she still holds for Magnus is what's keeping her alive. It's the only living thing about her— the cause of whatever breath she has left in her decrepit body. Her heart… it's still beating with that love, even after all this time."

Everyone was speechless for a moment as we let the witch's words sink in.

"So what exactly are you saying?" Xavier asked. "We'd have to kill Magnus?"

Mona shook her head. "We don't need to kill

Magnus."

"Then what?"

"We need to break Lilith's heart."

Chapter 38: Rhys

I stared at the giant mound of rubble where our castle had once stood. I knew who must have done this. But there was no time for anger now. I looked around at my comrades, then at the latest batch of young humans we had gathered.

We wouldn't have much use for that castle soon anyway.

In a matter of days, our ritual would be complete and if Lilith held up her side of things, we would be abandoning both our islands here in the human realm. The Sanctuary would be our new base and, once settled there, we would create gates directly into the human realm to collect blood whenever we needed it.

I supposed that whatever witches had been in the castle when the dragons attacked would have escaped— likely back to our base in the supernatural realm.

I locked eyes with my aunt. We both nodded, understanding each other.

"Julisse," I said, now turning to my sister. "Take these humans through the gate. If it's too burdensome to uncover the one here beneath the rubble, just use the one in Stellan's old island. As for the rest of us, we'll head right back to human shores. We still have more young blood to harvest."

My commands were obeyed. Julisse turned her back on me and prepared to start herding the adolescents while the rest of us vanished.

When we reappeared again, we were standing a dozen feet away from a tall brown building. Above the door was a sign that read *Woods Home Orphanage.*

As we approached the building, I visualized in my mind—as I had done a hundred times already—the ritual being successful. I pictured the thousands of Ancient spirits surfacing from their graves. Of course, they would not remain with us forever—it was impossible to truly bring a person back from the dead. But even as spirits they would possess enough power to breathe life back into our kind and reinstate our dominance. And this time, even if it meant sacrificing every human and other being lesser than us, we would make sure it stayed that way.

READY FOR THE FINAL BOOK IN ROSE & CALEB'S STORY?

A Shade of Vampire 16: An End of Night is the thrilling finale of Rose and Caleb's series!

An End of Night is available to order now.

Please visit www.bellaforrest.net for details!

Also, if you'd like to stay up to date about Bella's new releases, please visit: www.forrestbooks.com, enter your email and you'll be the first to know.

an end of
night

A Shade of Vampire, Book 16
BELLA FORREST

A Note About Kiev

Dear Shaddict,

If you're curious about what happened to Kiev during his time away, how he met Mona and how he came upon Anna, I suggest you check out his completed stand-alone trilogy: *A Shade of Kiev*.

Kiev's story will also give you a deeper understanding of the Shade books and the kind of threat the Novaks are now up against.

Please visit my website for more details: www.bellaforrest.net

Best wishes,
Bella

CPSIA information can be obtained at www.ICGtesting.com
Printed in the USA
LVOW08s1746050516

486865LV00008B/842/P